SOMETHING FISHY THIS WAY COMES

Books by Gabby Allan

Much Ado About Nauticaling

Something Fishy This Way Comes

SOMETHING FISHY THIS WAY COMES

GABBY ALLAN

Kensington Publishing Corp.

www.kensingtonbooks.com

KENSINGTON BOOKS are published by

Kensington Publishing Corp.
119 West 40th Street
New York, NY 10018

ISBN: 978-1-4967-3109-8 (ebook)

ISBN: 978-1-4967-3107-4

First Kensington Trade Paperback Printing: August 2022

10 9 8 7 6 5 4 3 2 1

Printed in the United States of America

This book is dedicated to all my fellow authors! Keep writing those stories and keep mining those imaginations. The world needs more of our hope and entertainment.

Acknowledgments

A huge shout-out to my critique partners in crime and to Esi Sogah, my amazing editor, as well as the copy editors who make me not only a better writer with better books, but a better person. Thank you from the bottom of my heart! This book rocks because of you.

Author's Note

Hey there, readers! Just a quick note to clarify that I am fully aware that I've taken liberties with how the coroner's office works with Catalina Island and that the body would normally have been transferred to the L.A. Examiner's office for the autopsy.

We're going to pretend that with the labor shortage and the method of death that my way is at least possible in my fictionalized town. Thanks!

SOMETHING FISHY THIS WAY COMES

Chapter 1

"So I told Aaron Franklin that there was no way he'd seen an island loggerhead shrike because they just don't like to be seen, and you know what he said? That for a twitcher I was more of a twit. How do you like them clamshells, Whit?"

For the seventh time in five minutes (and yes, I'd counted) I rolled my eyes as I stared down at my receipts for the day. The older man had said he was here for a gift for his granddaughter's sixteenth birthday, but he had yet to do anything more than lean on my counter and talk my ear off. He stopped in a few times a week to shoot the breeze, and normally it was okay, but not today.

Running a boutique gift shop on the small island of Santa Catalina, off the coast of California, had been my dream and still was, now that the Dame of the Sea was actually up and running, but I hadn't necessarily considered the fact that I'd always have to be nice to the locals. Even the ones who irritated me. And I couldn't kick them out just because I had things to do. Well, not unless it was closing time, which was why I was watching the clock.

Ten more minutes and I could get rid of Manny Jackson and his bird stories of twitching rivalry with another resident on the island. The guy never seemed to run out of stories that constantly cast him in a great light while leaving others looking like underwater barnacles. Or at least that was his intention. In truth, that was rarely how it came across.

"We compared our notebooks of finds the other day, and he didn't even have a bald eagle on there. Calls himself a twitcher. Not hardly. Right? He's not a twitcher, right? I should tell him that again, shouldn't I?" He scoffed and thumbed the side of his nose when I didn't answer right away. I was not going to get in the middle of that argument.

The wrinkles on his forehead and the graying combover very clearly showed he was of an age where he thought he could do or say anything he wanted. And of course he could, but just maybe not in my store.

If I'd had customers in my little shop of baubles, I'd have shooed him out. But since few people had come in today, I didn't have an excuse.

"You have to have specific birds to be considered a twitcher?" Not that his conversation had any value to me, but with only seven minutes left, it might make good business sense to interact. He was an infrequent customer, but a customer nonetheless.

Although I had a feeling at this point though that I was going to be ushering him out of the store without one of my gift bags.

"Oh, now, I don't know about specific, but there are some that are just common sense to have in there." He went on to list all the birds that were must-haves.

Of course he did.

I tuned back out until the front door opened and salvation came zooming into the store in the form of my best friend and roommate, Maribel Hernandez.

"Hey, Maribel, hey." There was definitely an edge of desperation to my voice, and I didn't even try to hide it. "Are you ready to go get something to eat?" I glanced at my clock. Three minutes left.

When I looked back up she had shock and dismay on her face and her hands were clutched together. "We're not having dinner tonight, Whit—or are we? Did I forget? Oh, man, I hope I didn't forget. I have a date tonight, but I can cancel it if you need me to."

And just like that she went from happy to worrywart in two point four seconds. I called it her spiral. Usually it wasn't that big of a deal and was easy to get her out of. But recently she'd had a lot on her mind with working the front desk at the police station and going to school for criminal justice, and I didn't want to add to it by making her think she'd forgotten me.

"Slow down, slow down. No need to get in a bunch," I said.

"But if I was supposed to do something with you . . ." She wrung her hands until her knuckles turned white.

"It's fine."

"But it's not."

"Maribel."

Poor Manny was turning his head at a breakneck speed to keep the speaker in his line of vision. He looked like he was watching a ferocious tennis match instead of a conversation between friends that had gone awry. And how had it gone awry?

Oh right. I'd tried to lie and that never went well for me.

"Yes?" she said and then both she and Manny looked expectantly at me.

Fortunately, I was saved from saying anything else because Manny's phone jingled in the breast pocket of his short-sleeved Hawaiian shirt.

When he opened his ages-old flip phone, he held up a finger to let us know it was time for silence. "What do you want, Aaron Franklin, you old sea dog? I don't have time for your shenanigans." He cocked his head to the side as the person on the phone answered his question. "You didn't!" Manny exclaimed. "You codger! You never did see an ashy storm petrel. That's my bird, the one I've been looking for. You're lying to me. They're on the watch list and you darn well know it." Another pause where he wiped his brow and squinted his eyes as if he were in pain.

Was he going to have a heart attack? Should I call the emergency responders? I looked over at Maribel, but she looked as baffled as I was.

"I'll be right there!" Manny barked into the phone, loud enough for several people strolling along the sidewalk out front to turn their heads to look in my quaint little shop.

"You'd better have pictures," Manny continued. "And don't you dare scare that thing off. If you *are* lying to me, I'm going to hang you by your binoculars from the nearest tree. Wait for me." With that he snapped his clamshell phone closed. There was no prying that thing away from him no matter how old it was. He didn't like new technology.

"Gotta go," he said, turning back to us. "Aaron, the rascal, says he saw a bird I've wanted in my book for ages, and he'd better be able to prove it before he puts it in that darn book of his."

"Aaron who you were just complaining about? The one who called you a twit? Why would he even call you?"

"That one exactly. That whole family is a little squirrelly, if you don't mind me saying so. But that's not going to stop me from seeing what he's got out there at the golf course."

"But if you don't like him, why do you do that?" I asked. "Can't you go catch the view of the bird without interacting with him?"

"Girl, I said I didn't trust him and he was squirrelly, not that I didn't like him. Yeesh, us birders have to stay together. No one understands us like we do. We might not always see things the same way, but that doesn't mean I walk away from my brothers. Unlike those Aherns, our mayor being the worst of the lot."

Okay then, I thought as he took off out of my store, slamming the door closed behind him.

Maribel raised one dark eyebrow. "What on earth was that?"

"Your guess is as good as mine, but hopefully Aaron really

saw whatever bird he was taunting Manny with, or there's going to be a very steep price to pay. Death by binoculars. I don't think that would be a peaceful way to go."

Maribel snorted. "Yeah, I'd rather go quietly in my sleep. Just not anytime soon. And if you don't get involved in anything else that's none of your business then we should be fine."

"That was not my fault, and it's been weeks since I fell down that ravine as I raced to find a killer." Actually, I'd been pushed, but we didn't talk about that. I closed the receipts on the computer and then gave her my full attention. "So why did you come by? I thought you had things to do this afternoon."

"What about dinner? Did I really miss that or were you just trying to get rid of Manny?"

She knew me too well. I shrugged while flashing my teeth in my best smile, and she laughed at me.

"You had me there for a minute. I really thought I had forgotten. With going to school and trying to keep up with my work schedule, I'm forgetting all kinds of things, so it wouldn't have surprised me if I'd forgotten a dinner."

"Nah, it was just to get him to move along." I looked at the clock on the wall, decorated with the mountains on the island and the ocean spread out along the bottom like a carpet. "But I do have to get going. I have a chest to deliver, and I want to get it out of the way so I can go rest. It's been a long day, even though I don't feel like I did much of anything."

My receipts said as much. I was going to have to give some serious thought to upping my game. My grandmother, Goldy Dagner—whose real name was Georgiana, but nobody called her that for fear of annoying her—kept trying to get me to sell different things, but I had had a specific dream when I'd opened this place and it didn't involve carrying a menagerie of scents and soaps. I wanted to keep most of my stock handcrafted items from the locals, but I wasn't selling as well as I'd like.

"Enough about me," I said, not wanting to think about selling and money right now or I'd go into my own spiral. "What did you need from me that had you bustling in here all smiles before I attempted to ruin it with my inept lies?"

"Oh!" She gripped her hands together in front of her chest and rocked back and forth. "I have a date."

"Yep, you mentioned that."

She snorted in laughter. "Fine, then, I'm sure I didn't tell you who it was."

"Nope."

"Fabian Halston." She squealed and I barely held in a groan.

Ugh. I glanced at the clock again and realized I should have closed the store two minutes ago. I did not have the time to drag her through the hours of reasons he was not a candidate for actual dating and hadn't been since we'd both been teenagers. And as far as I knew, he hadn't changed. Regardless of the fact that he was hotter than an August afternoon, he was also as dangerous as not taking your trash with you after you visited with the buffalo on the other side of the island. Since that was a protected area, you had to take it back out if you brought it in unless you wanted to pay dearly.

But this was my best friend. I couldn't let her walk into this one blind.

I was wondering how she'd never heard the gossip about him—or if she had and just didn't care—and was in the process of coming up with the best way to tell her to stay the hell away from the guy when Goldy walked in.

"Fabian Halston—" I began.

Goldy, in her usual way, cut me off with a flourish of her knee-length, see-through swimsuit cover-up. Always dressed for the beach, that was my grandmother. This one was royal purple and left little to the imagination. "Oh girl, you need to stay away from that one. He's trouble and never hesitates to let you know it with that cheeky smile and those reaching hands. Takes after his uncle Milo as far as I'm concerned. He's an Ahern through and through, even if his mother tried to pass him off as a Halston."

"Manny was just in here complaining about Mayor Milo. He's related to Fabian?" How did I not know that? You'd think on an island with a little over three thousand permanent residents, I'd know who was who and who was related to whom.

"I don't know what Manny was complaining about, and I really don't care. I just stopped in to let you know we have a delivery coming in tomorrow. And before you fight me, let me say that I paid for it with my own funds and am willing to let you take it on consignment. So be nice to the deliveryman, and I'll be in to unpack the shipment. Don't open it without me." Then with a flip of her purple cover-up, she was back out the door again, just like the small tornado I thought of her as.

"Now what was *that* all about?" Maribel asked.

"To be honest, I have no earthly idea. But I've been trying to hold in my groan about the guy you want to date, and I just can't do that, not if I really want to call myself your friend. He's not really a good guy."

She brushed her hand through the air as if whisking away my comment. "He doesn't have to be *the one*, Whitney Dagner. I can just have an interesting conversation and a good meal out of it. I'm not against exploring my options."

Putting a hand on my heart, I feigned hurt. "Don't I give you good conversation? And my spaghetti last night was absolutely divine."

With her hands on her hips, she laughed at me. "Yeah, and I had to share it with your adorable boyfriend, Felix, who I envy you for but don't expect to get one of my own anytime soon. However, my choices are limited at the moment. I can't exactly go out with anyone from the police department right now if I want to be taken seriously. And while I like to take in the town by myself, or with you, I'd really like to hang with someone else who sees things from a different perspective."

"Hmm. Well, you'll definitely get that with Fabian. Just don't be angry if he's not worth the time for the conversation, and make sure he at least pays his portion of the bill before he steps out to take a nonexistent phone call. It's his M.O."

She snorted. "Fine, I've been warned. I know all about guys like that. Now I have to get going if I'm going to battle your cat for space in the bathroom and wrestle my curling iron away from her long enough to get ready for my date. Be careful with that treasure chest you're burying. I still can't forget what happened up at the sanctuary."

I couldn't either and worried about it sometimes. "It" being finding another body. But there hadn't been another murder in weeks and Catalina Island was a relatively safe place.

"I've been properly warned also, then. I'm just hoping I don't run into Manny and Aaron in the middle of a fight over twitching."

Famous last words.

Chapter 2

After picking up my lovely (but rascally) cat, Whiskers, from my house, I drove my golf cart over to the golf course up the hill. I figured giving Maribel the time and the cat freedom to get ready for her date was the least I owed her since said date was probably going to be awful. It shouldn't be made worse by looking bad.

Whiskers enjoyed being out and about. There was no reason she couldn't just come with me since I had to deliver and bury the treasure chest I'd promised to Betty Blakefield for this afternoon. The woman was surprising her husband, Grant, with some kind of dream vacation and had wanted to do a treasure hunt to prolong the anticipation.

I, of course, was totally on board with that, though I wasn't always very keen on hiding things out by the golf course. I didn't want anyone to accidentally get nailed with a stray golf ball when following the map my grandfather, Pops—Thomas Dagner—had made.

But that map was one of our best sellers and he loved the thing. So I had recommended it when Betty requested something that would take about an hour to find.

I'd seen Betty and her husband walking by the shop while

Manny was complaining on the phone to Aaron, so I had about another thirty minutes before they came out my way. Just enough time for me to get this thing buried and then get out of the way so I wasn't here for the big reveal.

Parking at the entrance to the golf course, I sat for a second in my flashy autoette, with its stickers and spray paint art, and took out the master map from Pops. I ran my finger over the part of the map for the golf course and found the big red X at the end of the dotted line. A soft breeze ruffled my short hair and brought the smells of the sand and sea to my attention. I closed my eyes, just for a second, to enjoy both scents. So very different from the smog and diesel I'd left behind when I'd moved here from Long Beach.

I'd need to head across the eighteenth hole and go just underneath the trees management had planted at the edge of the green. Hopefully, I could get in and out without encountering too many people. Few carts were parked in the lot with me, although that didn't always mean anything. Almost anyone in Avalon could walk here. Heck, they could walk just about anywhere on the island if they had the time and the desire. The fewer golfers, though, the happier I'd be.

After clicking on Whisker's leash, I stepped out of the golf cart and let her frolic as we walked through the artificial turf. She rolled, she clawed, she attempted the downward-facing dog pose to stretch out her spine, and then she trotted. Sometimes I was convinced she thought she was a dog. She'd never pranced, but she was only a few years old. There was still time for that at some point.

The trek wasn't far, so I used the time to run through the things I had planned for the rest of the week. Dinner with the grandparents and Felix tonight, inventory over the next few days, and apparently accepting a delivery for Goldy, the grandmother who refused to be called any such thing. When my brother, Nick, and I were younger, we'd tried a host of different names for our only remaining grandmother, but she would have none of it and constantly corrected us with "Goldy" until it stuck.

Whiskers and I were at the last bend before the area I was looking for would come into sight, and I wanted to make sure I wasn't going to get hit by someone's overzealous or off-target stroke.

Glancing up, I zeroed in on the location, but instead of just a tree with a small place for a hole in the dirt at the base where I normally buried the box to be found by the customer, I found myself staring at a screaming match between Manny and Aaron, standing next to Aaron's golf cart.

I should never have thrown that out into the universe. She'd probably taken it as a challenge and told the moon to hold her beer.

The closer I got, the more I didn't think they were fighting, though. Manny appeared to be trying to calm Aaron down as Aaron wrapped the strap of his binoculars around his own neck and pulled until I thought he might pop his head off. So, Manny wouldn't have to hang him by his binocular strap since Aaron was apparently trying to do that all by himself.

Dropping the treasure box at my feet, I ran, dragging Whiskers behind me even as she yowled indignantly. Oh my gosh, this was not good. Maybe Aaron was having a raging fit because he'd lost that ashy thing that he'd promised Manny.

Weirder things had happened, though I was having a hard time pulling anything up at the moment as my breath sawed in and out of my lungs. Running was not one of my strong suits. Beyond that, I also didn't want to hurt Whiskers in the process, and she darted away from me every time I tried to snatch her up. But I hoofed it as best I could over a small rise and up to the pair standing just outside the tree line.

Once I got close enough to make out their words, I didn't understand what was going on any better.

"Aaron, knock it off. This is manageable. You don't have to do anything but breathe, and you can't do that with those damn things pulled tight around your neck." Manny made a grab for the binoculars and Aaron sidestepped him and then fell backward. The turf was pretty flat here as far as I knew but maybe he'd just tripped over his own feet.

Except when I looked closer, I saw a third guy. This one was lying on the grass, staring up at the sky with unblinking eyes, blood trickling out of his mouth. He'd been hidden from my view by the golf cart, and I wished he'd stayed that way.

I so did not want to find another corpse. It had only been a few weeks since the last one had floated underneath my brother's glass-bottom boat. To say I didn't want a repeat of any kind was a serious understatement.

"What happened?" I asked both men. But they were still yelling at each other, so I turned my back on them. There were more important things to deal with. Fighting my severe trepidation, I reached down and touched the man's neck. I avoided looking into his eyes because I just couldn't face that blank stare right now. But I knew who he was.

I found no pulse and checked again just to be certain before I made the call I dreaded.

This was not good. Leo Franklin, a young guy who had just moved back to the island a few months ago to get his life in order, was gone. We'd been friends with him and his family for as long as I could remember. He was Aaron's nephew, if I remembered correctly. And now he was dead. But how had it happened?

It didn't matter. We needed the police here now. I would deal with Manny and Aaron later. I whipped out my cell phone from my back pocket. As I swiped the screen to make the emergency call, someone came pounding up behind me.

Manny? Or a more sinister character? Maybe Aaron had killed his nephew and didn't want me to tell anyone. Is that what Manny had meant when he said this was "manageable"?

I didn't want to look but I also didn't want to get jumped from behind or caught unaware. My imagination went wild as I pivoted, thinking I might find a killer at my back. But no, it was Jake Ahern, one of the island's park rangers.

"Oh, thank goodness, you're here. I just saw him and came running." I was still a little out of breath, so I leaned forward with my hands on my knees and Whiskers pacing at my feet. She didn't stay there long and started batting at the poor dead man's untied shoelace.

I tried to drag her away, but she was having none of it.

Jake looked down at her, then up at me, then over at the two men who had finally stopped yelling at each other. "You might want to move away. I've got this taken care of."

"Okay." I didn't need to be told twice, though I did still have my phone out. "I can call it in for you if you want."

"No need, I already made a call when I saw him. It's a shame." He shook his head and I nodded. A terrible shame.

Manny had his arm around his friend, talking to him in a low voice. I wanted to go ask them what they'd seen or done. I stopped myself at the last moment because I thought I should either wait for the police or leave the questioning to Jake. However, he made no move toward the duo.

"You can go, Whit. I've got this covered. There's not much for you to do here." He stepped forwarded and fingered a piece of paper pinned to Leo's light blue jacket. "Suicide note. That answers that, then."

But did it? Leo was a fun guy, had recently returned to the island, had a ton to live for, and, from what I'd heard, had just started dating an island transplant. Why on earth would he have killed himself, and how was Aaron involved?

I looked at the body again and saw faint tire tracks across the chest of the jacket.

Uh-oh.

Had Aaron run him over? But then Leo would have already been lying down for Aaron's cart to go over him like that. So was he already dead, and Aaron hadn't seen him and run him over by accident, adding insult to injury?

Jake was shooing me away, though, and asking me to step over to the other side of the golfing green. Apparently, there was nothing more for me to do here. Except call the Blakefields and let them know I'd have to provide a new map and a new location.

Suicide or not, the cops would be swarming. And sending a customer out to try to dig under a dead guy was not optimal when it came to the big reveal of a dream vacation.

I did as I was asked by moving about ten feet away. Since my cell was still in my hand, I used it to call Betty Blakefield. A text might have been enough, and I certainly preferred those, but I wanted to try to catch them before they got here.

Betty picked up on the first ring. "What's going on?" she asked.

Thankfully, I had prepared my answer before dialing. "We've had a change in plans. Something's happened at the golf course. I'm going to have to move you to another location. Can we meet at the beach for me to give you a new map? I'll only need thirty minutes to get things into place."

The low-key noise of a bunch of golf carts converging over the hill had me raising my head. Whiskers yowled and clawed at my sock, but I ignored her to see what was going on.

People, a lot of them, stepped out of a bunch of carts parked on the eighteenth hole. I know it seemed to be the theme for the day, but really, *what the heck was going on?*

The crowd converged on Jake, in what looked like a sea of jet-black hair and sunbathed skin. From young to old, each one had a resemblance to one another that there just was no denying. And the more I looked, the more I started putting names on all of them. And every single one was an Ahern. Every. Single. One.

Well, maybe not the caddies who were driving them, but all of the golfers were Aherns.

My *what the heck* was ascending to a *what the hell* when they all turned to look at me and it was like a reverse image of *Children of the Corn*. Instead of all towheaded children, this was a group of dark-haired men, staring at me with hard expressions on their faces. I took a few more steps back, told Betty I'd meet her at the beach, picked up my cat, and then decided to skedaddle.

"Let me know if you need anything," I called back over my shoulder and left the grounds as quickly as I could, passing another handful of people making their way to the crime scene. Hopefully, Manny and Aaron would be able to explain what had happened. I had nothing to add to the information they probably had and no real reason to be involved.

That didn't stop me trying to figure out what had happened while waiting for the sirens of the police to come up the road. We weren't that far from the station and, really, unless there was something else huge going on that I hadn't heard of, they should have been here by now.

Another group of golfers and caddies passed me. This one was a mess of smells that nearly overwhelmed my nose. From dark cologne to light musk, they seemed to have it all, even a subtle floral undertone that reminded me of sunshine and creamy flowers. No one turned as they all swaggered to the final hole, the current resting place of a man who should be up and walking around.

I couldn't go back over to the site without being seen, and I had to meet Betty with a new map, but none of the carts that had pulled up to surround Jake had returned just yet. That made me wonder some more and take my phone back out.

Placing a call to Maribel was my best bet for finding out info without getting myself involved. So, I did.

"You're lucky he hasn't shown up yet, Whit." Maribel sounded disgruntled, and it took me a moment to remember she was supposed to be on a date with Fabian.

"Yikes, sorry on both accounts. I wasn't thinking."

"Well, now that you have me, keep me entertained until he shows up so I at least don't look like an idiot sitting at a table at La Annaffiare by myself. I've been putting the waiter off for twenty minutes now. I'm going to have to order something soon or get thrown out. I don't suppose you want to come down and join me? The bartender just handed out a round of free drinks so I have a couple more minutes before I have to go or order."

I bit my bottom lip before answering. "I'm sorry, Maribel, I can't tonight. I have plans. But you could get a quick dessert and then join me at the grandparents' house with Felix."

A big sigh blew through the phone. "No, it's okay, but dessert sounds about right at the moment." Another sigh made me want to go save her from being by herself at one of the priciest restaurants on the island, but I couldn't.

"I'm sorry."

"Well, at least you didn't say you told me so."

"I would never."

"Now come on, you have before, so it's not like it would be the first time. Anyway, you obviously had something you needed to ask me, or tell me, so spill. What's up?"

Did I want to get involved? Not that I was really getting involved. I was just asking a question. Right? Right.

So, it was okay for me to ask her if the cops had been called. I still hadn't heard any sirens. That was making me nervous enough to actually consider going back and facing the censure of the crowd just to make sure they didn't move the body or something.

"Come on, Whit, spit it out."

"So, you know how I was delivering a treasure chest?"

"Yes."

"Okay, and that was out at the golf course." I picked at some lint on my shorts. Not that there was eye contact to avoid when using the phone, but I couldn't seem to help myself from not looking up.

"Yes." This one was a little more drawn out like she was losing patience with me and/or was suspicious of the way I was telling or not telling the story.

"And so when I drove out to bury the chest, I took Whiskers. You remember, right? Because I wanted to give you time and space to do your hair?"

"Okay. At what point are you going to tell me what you need?"

"I don't have to tell you anything if you're going to get huffy," I said, then immediately wanted to take it back. "Sorry, I'm just nerve-racked and not sure what to do."

"Let's start over then," Maribel offered. "You found another body, didn't you?"

Hesitating, I bit my lip again and then let it go before I drew blood. "Yes. When I went to bury the treasure, I found Aaron Franklin and Manny yelling at each other over Leo Franklin's body. He has tire tracks on his chest, Maribel, and Aaron is the only one who had a golf cart out there. But then Jake Ahern, the park ranger, showed up and said he was going to call the right people. Except I still haven't heard any cops pull up and a whole platoon of golf carts are there and everyone looks alike." There, I'd spilled it all. Now I just had to wait to see what she had to say.

It didn't take her long. "Did you call the police?"

"No, I didn't want to seem to be getting involved when Jake already told me he'd take care of it."

"I've gotta go. I'll be down there in a few minutes. I'm calling in the cavalry first."

She hung up on me, but I forgave her as I sat in my autoette and wondered what to do next. When Whiskers meowed to my right, I turned to comfort her. In the process I saw Felix Ramirez, my boyfriend, walking toward me through the parking lot.

Felix Ramirez, my *police-diver* boyfriend.

"Dare I even ask what it is that you're doing here, Whit? Or would that take a lot of time to explain when there's a dead body over the ridge?"

Chapter 3

There was something to be said for a little mystery in a relationship. But as this was our third dead body in less than six weeks, I could have done without this particular kind of mystery.

I wasn't sure how to answer his question, or even what to tell him without sounding like I was where I shouldn't be. Just in time, the cops started showing up without their lights on or the sirens going. Did Maribel tell them to go in silent to catch all the people who I assumed were still standing around talking with Jake about who knew what?

I shrugged instead of answering Felix's question, and he gestured for me to follow him. Briefly, I considered leaving Whiskers in the cart and just tying her leash to the metal bar, but that probably wouldn't go very well, especially if she started yowling. I picked her up and held her instead of letting her walk. I didn't need the trouncing around she'd done earlier.

We followed closely behind the cops, but not too closely. Deputy Ryan Franklin looked back at me a few times, so I slowed my steps even more. Though Felix was a diver for the island force, he wasn't officially a part of the actual team and was only called in when needed. In his off time from the force, he gave private diving lessons and took people on tours underwater.

He was enjoying himself immensely from what he'd told me, and I was thankful because he'd followed me out here from the mainland, even though I hadn't invited him officially. The last thing I had wanted was for him to be disappointed at the choice he'd made regardless of whether I had asked him or not.

Before we came around the bend, the cops split up and went in two different directions.

"Are they trying to come up behind the crowd?" I asked quietly, not wanting to alert anyone.

"I really have no idea. I'm not even sure why I'm here other than Maribel texted me to let me know I needed to come keep you out of trouble until she got here."

Nothing like not being trusted to keep my nose out of things. I had no intention of getting involved. I hadn't wanted to get involved last time either, but that decision had ultimately been taken out of my hands. This time, though, I was going to make more of an effort to not be drawn in.

Or so I told myself. And I'd tell Felix and Maribel too if either of them asked.

In the meantime, there was a brouhaha brewing just around the curve and a trio of dark-haired men came running toward us. They didn't see us until it was too late, and Felix stood in the middle of the path so they couldn't pass.

"I have a feeling the cops would like to speak to you three. I wouldn't go getting into your vehicles until you've had a chance to talk with them."

They stopped in their tracks at Felix's words, but a fourth was coming up fast behind them and looking back as he barreled along the green grass. He ran smack into the trio and they all tumbled to the ground. Served them right.

"I'll just escort you four back the way you came, if you don't mind." Felix hadn't moved and appeared to be a wall they couldn't get around.

There was grumbling and a choice word or two, but they

complied. For my part, I followed along right behind with a purring Whiskers in my arms.

I should have brought popcorn.

Too late for that, but it wasn't too late to see the way the cops around Jake were puffed up, apparently waiting for some answers. I had no idea what the question was, but it almost had to be something to do with why he would have called his relatives instead of the cops when he'd found a dead guy. That was fishy even to me.

From the looks the cops were giving, they thought it was fishy too. I couldn't wait to hear who said what first.

Right now, it looked more like a standoff than any kind of interrogation, though. And Aaron and Manny still stood apart, either unseen by everyone or being ignored for the moment. I wasn't certain which, but I went to stand by them.

"All right, since no one seems to want to talk, we'll start with you, Jake. Care to tell me what happened here? Then you can tell me why we had to get a call through a third party about this situation." Ray Pablano was new to the force but, since he'd come over with years of experience in San Diego, he was a good one to lead the talks here. Or at least I hoped so.

Jake stuttered over his words and looked around, but no one seemed to want to help him now that they'd all been caught. Finally, he shrugged and spread his hands out before him like he had no answer. "This is a family thing. The feud is getting out of hand again."

One of the dark-haired relatives smacked him in the shoulder while frowning hard at him. For his part, Jake threw his hands into the air like he couldn't win, no matter what he did. My bet was on the fact that that was completely true.

Jake's comment very obviously did not sit well with Deputy Pablano, especially when Jake was the first one handcuffed.

"Fine, then, take them all down to the station and book them for aiding and abetting."

I opened my mouth to comment that I didn't think those were valid charges, but Felix threw me a look and shook his head with one sharp movement.

"What's the jail time for that, Mannon?" Pablano asked another man in uniform as they both put handcuffs on the men. I hoped they had extra pairs in the car.

"Ten to twenty, I think. We'll have to look it up while we're processing fingerprints and making sure no one has a warrant out for their arrest."

One of the men slunk back a few steps, hiding behind everyone else, and then turned tail and ran. Well, if it were me, I'd be looking at him first.

He didn't get far before he was stopped by one of the younger officers who probably went to the gym a lot. Why did people run? Especially criminals? Especially on an island? Did he really think he had any hope of getting away? Hardly.

Once they were all corralled together again, they were led back to the parking lot where everyone was divvied up and taken to the station. What I wouldn't have given to be a fly on the wall for that one.

Felix and I remained in the parking lot, where Maribel had finally arrived.

"Your date never showed?" I asked, placing a hand on her arm.

She laughed but it was more derisive than happy. "Actually, he did. He said he'd been sitting in the bar waiting for me the whole time. I don't remember seeing him, but then I didn't really look in the bar. He caught me on my way out after your phone call. I told him I'd have to take a rain check and then left."

"Who are you seeing?" Felix asked.

"No one at the moment," Maribel answered, shooting a look my way.

I shrugged in surrender. If she didn't want anyone else to know then I wasn't going to be the one to tell on her.

"Anyway," she continued, "I called the sheriff's office and

they were never contacted about this. Jake Ahern is going to have a lot to answer for. I want to be there for the interview but I doubt they'll let me."

"Oh, you should try, though. It would be good to have the information." Not that I was going to get involved, but that didn't mean I wasn't incredibly interested—and let's be honest, nosy—and I wanted to know what Jake had to say for himself.

"We'll see. I already ducked out on the date so I'm not going to go back and try to redo it. I guess I'll head home." She kicked at the dirt on the ground.

"You really can come to dinner with me and Felix at Goldy and Pops's. They'd love one more mouth to feed at the table. And maybe we could all talk this through. See what they have to say about Jake and the family gathering around a corpse."

She shook her head again. "Nah, I think I'm done peopling today. Whiskers and I will just hang out at the house. Unless you were planning on taking her with you to your grandparents' house?"

I laughed at that. Whiskers did relatively well outside or at our house but definitely not at Goldy's. With all those very tempting knickknacks and doodads on display that Whiskers just loved to knock over to see if anyone was watching, she irritated Goldy more than I was willing to risk.

"I'd love it if you took her home. I have to go deliver this chest to a new location and then go to dinner. If you could take Whiskers home so I don't have to also make that stop that would be awesome."

"Consider it done." She took the cat from my arms and the darn thing snuggled right into her shoulder. Though I'd rather they did get along, since we all lived together, her favoritism sometimes rankled. I was the one who fed her, you'd think she'd like me more.

"I'll see you later, then?" I eyed her up and down. "And if you hear anything, make sure you don't keep it to yourself."

Maribel had the gall to laugh and so did Felix, who'd been quiet for most of our exchange except for a grunt here or there and looking out over the golf course.

"I'll see what I can do." Maribel smiled at me, one of those secret smiles like she had something up her sleeve and couldn't wait to surprise me with it. I didn't like surprises, but I didn't have time to remind her of that before she hopped into her autoette with my cat and zoomed off down the road. It might have been impossible to chirp the tires at take-off in one of those things but Maribel certainly did try.

"Not going to get involved, huh?" Felix crossed his arms over his impressive chest and also had a smug smile on his face.

"Totally not getting involved, so you can stop smiling like that. I know when it's a job for someone else, but I just can't believe Leo would have killed himself. And where did the tire tracks come from? I highly doubt Aaron ran over him, even by accident. I thought Leo was getting his life back in order and had big things on the horizon. He had a lot of friends around the island and a good life, from what I could tell. Have you heard anything that would make you think this was his last option?"

"Nope, nothing from over here, but suicide isn't always about outward stuff. We'll have to wait to see what the police find out. Right now, though, we have dinner, and you have a chest to deliver. Do you want me to go ahead to Goldy and Pops's? You can just meet me there?"

"Would you mind? That way I can get this chest put into the ground and at least accomplish one thing today."

He kissed me on the forehead. "I'm sure you've accomplished much more than that. I'll see you around."

He too hopped into his autoette and motored off down the road, but not nearly as fast as Maribel. I took my time getting in my cart, then zoomed down to the beach.

It wasn't exactly the wind in my hair on the 405 Freeway with the top down, but it was good enough. With a speed limit not to exceed twenty-five on pretty much the whole island, and a golf cart that usually struggled to hit fifteen, you did what you could with what you had.

When I arrived at the beach, I found Betty and her husband surrounded by a group of people with light hair. It was a weird contrast to the dark-haired brood I'd seen earlier. But what were they doing? I thought I was only meeting her? Had something changed and I hadn't been notified?

"Hey, Betty!" I called over everyone's head. The sea of blondes parted to reveal her tear-stained face and her resolve.

"Put the chest wherever you want or just hand it to me. We need you for something much more important."

"What's that?" Though I had a sinking feeling in my stomach.

"We need you to infiltrate the Aherns and find out who killed our cousin." She gestured with a hand to the group behind her who were all nodding. "This family feud has gone too far now. If they're going to play dirty then we need to do the same thing, and you're the best person we can think of to show us the dirtiest of playbooks."

Chapter 4

Really? Me? A dirty playbook leader? I had never thought of myself like that, to be honest. And I wasn't entirely sure why anyone else would think that of me either. Asking why was out of the question because I was pretty sure I wouldn't like the answer.

Instead, I gave them my shrug with hands held out in gesture. "I'm not sure what you want me to do, or even how you think I would do it. Why would the Aherns let me in at all, especially now? And what's this feud about?"

They all kind of looked at one another and did minute gestures that felt like some kind of Morse code or hive mind.

"We'll talk about it later," Betty said, flapping her hands at the group like they were a gaggle of geese. "Right now, I have an amazing present for my husband to find! And I want him to know that I appreciated his secret nest egg so much that I did something with it that will last a lifetime!"

Her husband, Grant, choked and then smiled weakly. Betty whacked him on the back.

"You're going to love this so much, sweetheart. I can't wait for you to find the chest." Turning to me, she beamed with pride. "Now go hide that thing so we can get on our way. I'll figure out how you can help us in the meantime, and we'll get to the bottom of who killed my cousin. Those Aherns won't get away with it. No way did Leo kill himself. You'll show them it isn't true."

She seemed so sure of herself that I didn't have time to get into an argument with her and still get this chest buried in time to make it to my grandparents' house for dinner so as not to leave Felix hanging with them by himself for too long.

Perhaps while I was digging up dirt in the ground, I could figure out how to not get caught up in digging up dirt on a family that had been on this island almost since the town was founded.

I didn't hold out a ton of hope for that, but I did hand over the map with a smile that might have been more of a grimace and then went on my way over to the deer sanctuary just outside the historic Catalina Casino. It was another popular spot and one that wasn't too hard to get to. Not to mention it was also close to where we were currently so I could get this done and get to dinner as soon as possible.

Suddenly I found myself very hungry for whatever Goldy had cooking, along with maybe some conversation that didn't involve murder or me solving another one. I hoped it was huli huli chicken—a sort of teriyaki-style dish—and Hawaiian macaroni salad on the table and small talk on their minds.

Putting the box under a hedge that I'd used numerous times over the last several months, I left it there and then texted Betty that it was ready when she was. With my job done, I jumped into my autoette and headed back into the hills surrounding Avalon Bay.

Moving to Catalina Island had been the best decision I'd ever made, but it hadn't been an easy one. You had to pay shipping on everything and anything you wanted brought to the island came over on a barge, unless you could carry it on a ferry.

I'd chosen the lightest couch I could find and pared down my wardrobe as best I could. Kitchen utensils that I'd had for years were replaced with plastic just so that the metal wouldn't cost me more than it was worth. I had replaced some of them from the grocery store once I'd arrived, then realized how much I did not like having only a plastic spatula for my tiny hibachi grill. But other than that I'd been careful with my money and my possessions.

I'd known when I'd moved here that it would be a close community. With three thousand residents I wouldn't say I knew everyone in town but I knew most of them. And most of them were good people.

But those few who weren't were easily handled, as far as I was concerned, by just staying away from them. And I planned on continuing with that idea. However, if I was going to get pulled into another investigation, then I was again going to be pulled into the underside of the island. Into the lives of people who weren't on their best behavior.

I got that everyone was human and that everyone had flaws, but there was a big difference between a flaw and killing someone. I had my very polarized views on that kind of thing. I was fascinated by true crime television but I didn't want to be living in it.

Since few trips on the island were actually long, I showed up at Goldy and Pops's house in just a few minutes. Felix was already there, hopefully making inane conversation with my grandparents instead of talking about the latest murder on the island. Since I didn't see my brother's autoette, I figured it was probably just the four of us tonight.

Despite worrying about the murder that had happened earlier, I hoped with all my heart that it would be a night of funny conversation about the dog next door or how my grandfather was making a new treasure map and he needed me to test it out. Hell, I'd take Goldy talking about this mystery shipment that I'd be receiving tomorrow.

I opened the door to the one conversation I didn't want to have, of course.

"And Whit found him? Another dead body?" Pops pounded his fist onto the table and shook his head. "She needs to stay away from that kind of thing."

"It's not like I went looking for it." I slammed the door behind me and stalked into the living room.

"Come now, darling, he's not saying that." Goldy rose majestically from her chair, then patted me on the arm. "He just wants to make sure you're safe."

I harrumphed and the old codger smiled at me. "I didn't say you went looking for it. I'm just saying you need to get a Spidey sense or a death-y sense and avoid anything dead from now on. We want you to stay around for a while, honey. The last one didn't go so well but you were safe at the end. I don't want to take a chance like that again."

Felix gave me a one-arm hug and whispered into my ear, "Don't believe them. They heard you pull up and started this out of the blue. They want you to look into it but think if they ask you that you'll say no. They're hoping for some reverse psychology."

He kissed me on the cheek before he pulled away.

Ha! And Betty thought *I* held the dirty playbook leader title. These oldsters were the masters. Not that I'd ever tell Goldy she was old. She'd probably annihilate me. Instead, I worked hard to keep the smirk off my face and decided to play their game. And I'd win, though I wasn't quite sure what winning looked like yet. I'd figure it out.

Sitting on the arm of Felix's chair, I swung my leg and inspected my nails. "Oh, I'm not getting involved at all. In fact, they're looking at it as a suicide so there's nothing to look into."

Goldy sputtered and Pops clamped a hand on her knee so she didn't fly out of her chair.

"This was not a suicide." Pops said the words clearly but so softly that I paid attention. "There is no way Leo Franklin would have killed himself. He finally had a lot of good things coming up in his future. Things he'd been working toward for months. He was turning his life around. To take his own life now is ridiculous to even contemplate. I'd prove it myself. It's that darned century-old feud."

Oh, Pops being involved would be a real problem and could get him into trouble. "Do you know what the feud is about? I talked with the Franklins and they brushed me off. I don't know how they could have hatred but no information to back it up."

For once, Pops looked helpless as he raised his hands and sought out Goldy. "Don't look at me," she said. "I don't know what happened either, just that it was big, and no one has forgotten the hatred even if they've forgotten the reason for it."

"Well, how am I supposed to have anything to start with if I can't get the root cause?"

"You'll figure something out, dear. You always do."

"Look, let's let the police handle it. They have plenty of smart people on the force here. Surely they'll be able to get to the bottom of things without our help." At least I'd like to hope so.

Then again, they'd needed my help last time before the murderer headed off the island free from the consequences of killing for money. I sat on the couch and thought about how I wanted to go about this. I had been asked to look into things, people seemed to be going out of their way to not follow standard procedures, and now I was concerned my elderly grandfather, who was fun but not always in the best of shape, would go out and hunt a killer all on his own.

Guess who was about to get involved? I sighed and my grandfather zeroed in on me with his gaze.

"You'll do this so I don't have to?" he asked.

"I don't know that I have a choice since everyone seems to think I have some magic deerstalker cap, even though we have had a perfectly competent police force for years. You've said so yourself on many occasions."

"It's not that I don't think they're competent, but they just haven't solved many murders. They're a rare occurrence around here, after all. Or at least they were. I'm just afraid they're going to see a suicide and not do anything else about it because it's open and shut. I don't want Leo to go out like that if it really was murder."

"And if it really was a suicide?"

Pops harrumphed but then shrugged. "If you can prove that he took his own life then I will make peace with that somehow, but I know it's not true. He had so many good things on the horizon. Why would he decide to check out now?"

It was a good question, one I would put on my list of things to ask once I got home. For the moment, I just wanted to enjoy dinner with my family, hang out with Felix, and talk about things that didn't involve death.

They tried, I know they did as we ate the beautifully marinated chicken I craved and macaroni salad that had just the right amount of sweetness, but inevitably it came back around to what was probably the talk of the island by now: Why Leo and why now?

Pops wasn't even subtle about it as he dug into the chocolate lasagna Goldy had "made."

"So, here's the thing . . ." He trailed off as he looked up, his fork loaded, the bite ready to go in. I willed him to do just that but he put his fork down instead. "Not a lot of people know but Leo was about to get married to a girl despite a whole lot of obstacles that were trying to keep them apart."

I hadn't seen Leo around town with anyone in the last few weeks, but that didn't necessarily mean anything. He worked a lot and maybe they went out when I was already in bed. But marriage? Already? "What? He'd just moved back. And he was just getting his life back on track after all the trouble he had with the law on the mainland. What's the rush?"

"Bah. You know how some people are, and if it kept him honest then I say go for it. They'd known each other since they were little. Went to school together. So, it wasn't that quick. Now, why would he give it all up at this point when he had a marriage to look forward to?"

"And who is this marvelous woman who turned the head of our dear Leo?" Goldy asked archly. "And why am I just now hearing about her?" She shoved another forkful of chocolate lasagna into her mouth, maybe to keep herself from saying anything more.

Uh-oh. Most people didn't take lightly to being left out of the loop, but Goldy was particularly hostile about that kind of thing no matter how many times she had done it herself.

"Oh, now, honey, don't get cranky. His uncle Aaron had asked me to hide a treasure chest for Leo's beloved and I happened to be in the vicinity when the two kids found it. Just wandering around, you know. Didn't mean to be there, of course, but then my curiosity got the better of me." Pops's smile didn't turn Goldy's fierce frown upside down at all. In fact, it only made it pull down the corners of her mouth even further.

"Ah," he said, quickly wiping his mouth and putting his napkin down on the table. He patted Goldy's hand, but she snatched it away and shoved another forkful of dessert into her mouth. I had a feeling Pops was going to get yelled at after Felix and I left.

I turned to my right just to see how Felix was doing since he hadn't said anything in the last few minutes, only to find him smiling. He was enjoying this exchange. I couldn't say I wasn't too since Pops always seemed to get away with everything and Goldy was usually the one with the secrets. The reversal was kind of funny. But laughing at this point would probably have made both of them turn their grumpiness and uncertainty to me, and I did not want to be that target. So, I kept quiet, just waiting to see what happened next.

"I was going to tell you . . ." Pops started and Goldy snorted to cut him off.

"We live in the same house. We're both retired. We see each other more often than not. I highly doubt you couldn't have found a moment while I was washing the dishes, or dusting, or straightening the living room to tell me. You know, all those things I do while I let you fill your boxes in the living room and make your maps with the ink and quill? You know, that one that just happens to splatter on the rug every once in a while?"

And here we went. This could devolve pretty fast so I needed to get them back on track. But what track was the real question. I didn't want to talk murder, I didn't want to talk about my grandfather's failings, and I didn't want to incite another argument.

"So tell me about this shipment for tomorrow, Goldy," I said, jumping in.

"You aren't going to get me off track that easily, young lady. We'll finish this one first, and then get to that one after we talk about how you're going to find out who killed Leo so that my husband doesn't have to go put himself in harm's way." She shot me a deathly glare, and I raised my hands in surrender. Though of course if she was worried about Pops putting himself in harm's way, why was it then okay to put me in that same line of fire?

"Now," she continued, "do tell about what you know, dear husband of mine, so that Whit can go run around and keep you from getting yourself hurt in the process. I know she can handle herself, she did it last time, but you, on the other hand, concern me."

I figured I could take that as a compliment and just roll with it, so I did.

"All I was going to say was that I found out who Leo was marrying, and it took me off guard, but then we had so many other things going on—"

"Like me cleaning ink off the rug . . ."

"Hey, now, I do that myself whenever I see it."

"Which isn't often since you really should get stronger glasses, but continue. Please."

It was like watching a ping-pong match, and I knew just how Manny felt when Maribel and I had been doing our own quick back-and-forth earlier at the shop. My word, was that only this afternoon? It felt like a year ago.

Pops groaned and threw his hands into the air. "Fine. Leo Franklin was going to marry Janina Heller, the niece of Sylvie Fellini."

"You have got to be kidding me! And you didn't take the time to mention that?" Goldy whisked in and took the rest of Pops's chocolate lasagna from him. "You don't get this back until you spill all the tea on what you know."

His face dropped and he twisted his napkin in his hand. "You know I would have gotten around to it eventually."

"When? After they were married? I pride myself on being in the know around here. If my own husband won't even tell me what he knows, then how am I supposed to stay on top of the local gossip?" Goldy stood with one hand on her hip and the other still holding his dessert. I didn't think she'd necessarily throw it away and keep it from him altogether but right now it seemed like more of a possibility than when she'd first taken it from him.

And there was the rub. She wanted to know all the things and his not telling her was going to probably be brought up for the next fifty years. She still talked about how he hadn't told her about a time my parents had decided to buy a boat and sail for a month. That was twenty years ago. Then again, they'd never come back, so that was probably a little bigger than who Leo was marrying.

Although I wasn't entirely certain why this was such a big deal. Janina was a wonderful woman who had been on and off the island, like I had been, for years. And her aunt Sylvie was a nice person who ran one of the best restaurants in town, La Annaffiare, where Maribel had almost been stood up this afternoon. Sylvie's linguine was something to worship. It never seemed to actually make it to a to-go carton to be reheated at home because I couldn't stop myself from eating it all right at the table before leaving the dimly lit room with its candles and ambience.

"I like Sylvie," I piped in.

"She makes me love Italian food in a way that I thought I'd only ever love in my mom's cooking. But it outshines even my mom's skills in the kitchen," Felix said with a grin. "But don't tell my mom that, or I'll never get another homemade tortilla."

Great, now I had something else to worry about. I wasn't exactly a whiz in the kitchen, and if I was up against Sylvie and his mom, Felix was bound to be disappointed.

"I won't tell her, but you'd better have her come over sooner rather than later. I think it might be time we met your parents." Goldy switched her attention to my boyfriend, making him squirm.

Ah, now Goldy was putting Felix on the hot seat. I didn't know whether to be happy about the subject change or feel pressured to take our relationship up another notch,

Felix's ears turned red and he gripped the edge of the couch. Okay, time to change the subject. Again.

"So, I'm still not sure why Leo and Janina marrying was an issue," I said into the melee.

"Because Janina is part of the Ahern family through Sylvie

and they've been fighting with the Franklins for years. Maybe it's a reversal on the classic Romeo and Juliet thing. The feud's been going on since the early nineteen hundreds. Maybe in this particular story instead of the main character killing himself, someone did it for him and took Leo out to keep the feud alive." Goldy set down Pops's dessert and stood with both hands on her hips. "Now how about using that Shakespearean degree to find out how to catch a killer before anyone else is hurt?"

Chapter 5

"You know Shakespeare never actually said what their family feud was about?" It was an inane statement and meant to derail the conversation from yet again turning to me doing the dirty work here.

Although apparently everyone thought I was all about the dirty work since that's precisely what the Franklins had thought I would do when they'd talked to me on the beach earlier. Why did everyone think I was some master sleuth when I barely even qualified as an amateur sleuth, even by television standards? I didn't even have the skills of the woman from *Murder, She Wrote*.

Everyone ignored me, so I tried again.

"Let me get this straight," I said. "Leo and Janina were on opposite sides of this feud, yet they'd loved each other for years but never stayed together because their families were feuding. Now, out of the blue, they were going to buck the system and get married anyway. But Leo supposedly killed himself before they could say their vows? Is that about it?"

"Except for a few details, yes, I'd say you have it right." Pops sat with his fork still in his hand, probably hoping that Goldy would give him his dessert back. The look in her eyes, though, told me that she probably wasn't going to back down.

Ha! I knew it well from past experience. Like that one time when she decided that the shirt I was wearing was too revealing for ninth grade. When I'd refused to change it, I never saw it again after I put it in the wash for her to clean. I still wondered where that thing was every once in a while. And I didn't cross Goldy if I could avoid it knowing that the cost could be high in doing so.

"And I still am waiting to hear when exactly you planned on telling me that." Goldy picked his chocolate dessert up from the side table out of his reach where she'd placed it and Pops had been eyeing it.

"Would it help if I said I was sorry and that I'll never with-hold information from you again?" Pops pleaded with his eyes, and I nudged Felix.

"Yes, it would."

"Can I have my dessert, then?"

"I haven't heard the apology. Asking doesn't make it actually happen."

Felix nudged me back because I had a habit of doing the same thing and it was something we had talked about before, my not actually apologizing even though I'd offered to.

Karma wasn't always the nicest of ladies when you needed her to be.

"I'm so sorry, my lovely. I will, of course, tell you all the things right when I know them from now on. In fact, if someone is going to 'spill the tea' to me, as you say, I will call you right in that instant, ask them to hold on to the pot, and then put you on speakerphone. That way you too can be privy to the information firsthand, and not have to wait for this old brain to make the connection that you should be told. In this way, you may con-tinue to be the queen of all gossip on the island."

She'd started putting the chocolate lasagna on the table at his first sentence but then took it back and headed into the kitchen as he finished. That stuff was heading for the trash, I guaranteed it.

"Wait, darling, wait!" He kicked back his chair in his haste to follow her. "I'm kidding, and there's more information that I just found out this afternoon if you bring back that deliciousness that you made. I promise it will be worth your while!"

From my vantage point on the couch, I could see Goldy hesitate with the plate over the open trash can. She wanted that information, but she also didn't want to back down.

"She's not going to be able to resist," Felix whispered in my ear. I nodded and waited.

After one more second, Goldy turned around in a huff with the plate of dessert intact and almost threw it down on Pops's place setting.

"This had better be good." She clamped her elbows to her side. For my part, I waited breathlessly to hear what he thought he had to barter with.

He took two bites of his food before Goldy stepped back into his space. "Okay, okay, geez, can't a guy enjoy the wonderful things his wife makes for him?"

"That would be much easier if you'd start talking. Now. Or you're going to be wearing it instead of eating it."

With that he laughed and pulled her in to sit on his lap. He kissed her hair, or seemed to, and she stayed where she was for a minute while they hugged.

"Are you serious?" she asked as she shot up from his lap. "You have got to be kidding me!"

"Absolutely not," he responded. "I heard it from the horse's mouth."

"Don't you dare," I finally said. "You can't just hide it from me too, if you think I'm going to do anything to save you from making mistakes. And, Goldy, you will not receive a shipment in the store tomorrow if you don't share." I'd learned from the best, even if I didn't often use the skill. Goldy was not amused, but I didn't care.

And then she laughed. "You always were a quick learner."

"In most things," I agreed, not willing to be sidelined. "Now, spit it out."

"It seems our Janina was not doing a stellar job at her aunt's restaurant no matter how good her table service is, and she's taken to moonlighting." Goldy tapped her chin. "But then it wouldn't really be moonlighting if she was doing it during the day instead of at night, would it?" Goldy stopped herself in her own tracks of wandering off subject. "Why didn't I know this?" she seemed to be asking herself so I didn't step in yet. "And what is she moonlighting, or daylighting, as? It's not like you can hide much on an island this tiny with a population this small."

"Darling, you can only be so many places and doing so many things at once." Pops shoveled more dessert in his mouth. At the rate he was eating, she wouldn't be able to steal any more of his food, and he obviously knew it. "I think you didn't know because it's been kept quiet." He took the last bite and patted his stomach. "I don't even know what it is that she's doing but that might be something you'll want to look into, Whit, when you get out there and start sleuthing."

Ugh, sleuthing. Last time I'd had a stake in the game and needed to find out who'd done it so that I could keep my idiot, but loveable, brother out of jail. This time it felt like I was just wading in because I could. The police were not going to be happy about that, no matter how I spun it.

"Look, I'm not making any promises. I didn't make them to the Franklin family either." I clamped my lips together after that last statement. Damn it, I had not meant to mention that I'd already been approached by the Franklins.

"Wait, what's this?" Goldy came for my dessert, and I raised my fork to stab as necessary. I was not above poking her with it if she even tried.

"Back off. I don't want to hurt you and this is trying my nerves. At least let me eat."

Even though her eyebrows were raised, she did back away, and I breathed a sigh of relief.

"When I went to bury that chest for Betty she had gathered most of her clan down at the beach, and they all pleaded with me to look into this. They're not sure the police will do their job either. For some reason, they think I own the 'dirty little playbook' on how to get things done. I'm not sure why, but there you have it."

"Well, of course you're going to help them, then. That's a better reason even than keeping your grandfather out of trouble. Betty's been my friend since before you were born. If she needs help, then we're going to give it to her."

Since I couldn't roll my eyes without getting in trouble, I closed them but still had my fork in my hand if I heard Goldy take one step closer. "I already said I wasn't making any promises, but I can at least ask around. You two have given me more than I could have wished for in the questions-but-no-answers category. I'll get on it first thing in the morning. At this point, though, I think it's time for me to go home and take Felix with me. We appreciate your hospitality, but we need to get going."

I turned to find Felix still only halfway done with his own plate of sugary goodness. I raised my eyebrows like Goldy had, and he shoveled the rest of the dessert into his mouth through his grin.

Heaven help me.

"You keep me up to date, you hear?" Goldy said as she got us two more pieces of the fabulous yummy goodness now that we'd apparently fallen in with her plan.

"I'll do my best."

"And I'll remind her," Felix said as he took delivery of the food.

After we left the house, I turned on him as soon as we closed the door behind us. "Really, that's all you have to say all night? I would have at least hoped that you would have been in there telling them to let your fellow police officers do their jobs instead of encouraging them to think I'm going to solve this by myself."

His smile was a little sly and put me on my guard. "Oh, it's not going to be by yourself. Maribel and I are already in too. She's been looking around while we've been at dinner."

"Why didn't I know this?"

"You're sounding an awful lot like Goldy. Are you sure you want to do that?"

I admit it, I smacked him in the arm. When he bobbled the dessert and laughed at the same time, I caught the container and then kissed him on the cheek.

"Your little tap didn't hurt at all. I've had worse from people that I'm teaching to save others from drowning. I've got thick skin."

I huffed out a breath and considered hitting him again, but he sidestepped away from me.

"I really do think you should look into this, though. I trust most of the people on the force, but something seems off here, and I'm concerned. If they solve it before we do, then we can at least say we tried, and no one can blame us for not getting there first. But if they let it slide as a suicide, I'm afraid that things will go downhill from there."

Apparently he was going from not saying anything to saying a whole bunch in one long string. "Do my grandparents intimidate you? Is that why you don't talk around them?"

He shrugged. "Pops and I talk all the time, but Goldy is a little frightening. Don't tell me that other guys haven't felt the same way."

"I've never brought another guy around them." I walked away quickly to avoid what I knew would be the next thing out of his mouth.

"Really? And why is that, Ms. Dagner?"

He'd been pushing for more time, more of a commitment. As far as I was concerned, we were monogamous, and I wasn't out looking for anyone else and neither was he. That was enough for the moment. I wasn't sure what more he wanted, and quite frankly I didn't want to know. On this one I was going to have to bend, though, or he might ask Pops in one of their many talks. I'd think about that bit of information later.

"If you must know, I've never dated anyone over here, and it was too much to ask my grandparents to come to the mainland when I lived there to meet someone who generally didn't last more than one or two months. And I certainly wasn't bringing someone like that to the island. This is my shelter. My place to feel safe."

"And I intruded without being asked." He caught up with me in a few steps and clasped my hand in his. "Are you sure you don't mind that I live here now? I know we talked about it before, but maybe you were just being nice? I can take it if you wish I had asked first."

I growled because out in the street in front of my grandparents' house wasn't exactly the place I wanted to have this conversation. But if we didn't have it now, then it might trail along behind us.

"I love having you here. I've told you that before. It's great, and I'm glad you're fitting in, and I like that you're in with my grandparents. This is just all totally new for me. And I'm trying to navigate a series of things all at the same time—a new business, a new home, a new life, and a relationship that's not totally new but different here. So you're going to have to bear with me while I sort through."

He kissed the back of my knuckles. "I hope you know I'm here, or not, for as much as you need."

"See, and then you're so nice about everything and understanding that it makes me feel like an idiot." I scoffed and I huffed out a breath even as Felix laughed.

"Are you telling me I'm too nice? Because I have to say that's going to be a first for me."

This time I just smacked him in the arm and laughed. Then I sobered up and asked the question burning in my brain. "Are we really going to do this? Look into the suicide as a murder? I'm nervous that we're going to get in trouble. And last time I got shoved down a hill and almost had a tumble off a cliff. I don't know if my brain can handle that again, much less my body."

Hooking his arm around my shoulders, he kissed me on the temple. "You'll have help this time if you'll let Maribel and me also look into things, and we'll keep you safe. Just ask some questions and use that clue sniffer of yours, and the rest will work itself out. And if the police figure it out first, then good for them."

"You say that like you're not part of the force." I nudged him toward our respective golf carts.

"I am, but peripherally and only when it involves a dive. I'm not really in the inner circle and probably won't ever be. I like most of the people, but I don't see it being a forever job. I'm actually signing on more diving students and am thinking about getting more involved with rescue training."

"Well, then maybe you can rescue me from this delivery that Goldy is having sent to my store tomorrow."

He laughed at that. "Yeah, remember when I said she intimidates me? I don't think I'm going to step into that one."

"But you'll step into a murder investigation when it might be a suicide and could be dangerous if it involves secrets people might want kept hidden?"

"Honestly, that seems like a safer bet than tangling with Goldy."

Fair enough. Now the next thing to decide was where to start.

Chapter 6

The ride home with Felix following me to the house I shared with Maribel was short but just enough time to wonder if I had lost my mind. Who did I think I was? I had no real experience with figuring out a murder unless you counted all the television shows I watched. I was trained to run an office and make sure shipments got from boats to trains to where they belonged. I'd taught myself how to run a gift shop and I was proud of that. But I wasn't an amateur sleuth, not even one of those television heroines who always seemed to pull it out in the end.

But in my new life, apparently, I was being cast in the role, and I'd probably do much better to step up and at least try than to just ignore it and hope no one noticed. Plus, I did have the help of my best friend and my boyfriend to depend on, so there was that.

And I had liked Leo. No matter how much trouble he'd sometimes caused when he was younger on the island, running wild and breaking curfews, or the more serious issues of drugs and running with the wrong crowd on the mainland, he'd been trying to turn his life around. If he'd died under mysterious circumstances, and not by his own hand, then he deserved justice. Not to mention the person who'd ended his life early deserved to be sent to jail for a very long time. If the police weren't going to do it, then I wasn't exactly the last person I'd choose to help out. Maybe second to last but not last. I hadn't done such a bad job when we'd had a couple of murders on the island a few weeks ago.

Felix parked behind me on our quiet street before joining me at the front door of my rental home. Maribel had something cranking on the TV inside. I couldn't tell if it was music or a show, but it was loud enough to make the knob vibrate under my hand a little when I went to open the front door.

Once the door was open, it was even louder. How on earth could she think with all that noise? I was fully aware I sounded like my grandparents when I was younger, but we weren't thirteen anymore.

"Maribel!" I yelled into the front room when I didn't see her. I headed toward the TV remote and the blessed volume button, but she emerged from the kitchen to the right and put her hand over mine.

She shook her head and pointed back to the kitchen. Since our place was small it wasn't hard to see that someone was in the kitchen, even if I couldn't tell who it was. Their back was turned to me and he or she had a hat on, no hair showing.

Suspect? Grieving almost-widow? Someone from the other family? Someone from the Franklin clan deciding that I hadn't moved fast enough and wanted to make sure to include Maribel in pressuring me to do their dirty work?

Was the music loud to drown out their words?

I thought I had gone through everyone it could be, so I was entirely surprised to find my brother sitting at my breakfast bar looking like he'd been sailed hard and put away wet after a storm.

"Uh, Nick, what the heck are you doing here? I thought you were on another of your trips to the mainland and we wouldn't see you for a few more days."

"I came home early when Goldy called and told me you were going to be looking into a murder again. Wanted to see if you needed any help. You can turn down the music now, Maribel. I don't think anyone is going to hear anything interesting and I'm getting a headache."

I nodded in agreement while Maribel went to lower the volume.

Oh, I so did not need help from him. I didn't need help from anyone else. It was going to be enough for Felix and Maribel and me to keep ourselves in the loop without tripping over one another. And my brother was not very reliable even in the most mundane of situations.

"We've got this. No need to have come home early. You can go back whenever you're ready and do whatever it is you do over there when you leave the running of the cruiser to Pops." I wasn't always sure what my brother was doing when he wasn't running his glass-bottom boat tours, but it involved him flying on and off island from Airport in the Sky, our tiny airport on the top of the mountain. The one with a runway that stopped right on the edge of a cliff and dropped into the sea, so I didn't fly very often. Give me a big boat and an hour and a half in the wind and sea mist anytime.

"No, I want to help. Goldy said you might need me."

I yet again resisted the urge to roll my eyes. At this rate *I* was going to get a headache. "And when exactly did Goldy call you?"

"About three hours ago."

Right after I'd found the body. She must have been pretty confident that I wasn't going to be able to stop myself from helping.

"All I'm doing is asking some questions, I'm not really looking into anything."

Maribel snorted and Felix covered his laugh with a cough.

I stamped my foot and then immediately felt foolish. I steamed ahead anyway. "For heaven's sake, it's not like I go out and look for these things. People bring them to me and I do the best with what I've got." I slapped my hands on my hips but that reminded me too much of Goldy and her after-dinner pose with Pops, so I folded my arms instead and cocked a hip.

"I'm not saying you look for them," Maribel said, all innocence as she sat next to my brother. "I just find it interesting that you were approached by two different sets of people to look into matters when it should be handled by the police."

"And I would be fine not being approached by anyone if it's all the same to you. But the pressure's there, and everyone seems to know my exact buttons to push to get me moving." I shoved my hands into the pockets of my shorts. "I haven't had time to really look into anything, but I do have a list of questions. The first being, what is Janina down at the restaurant moonlighting as?"

Maribel picked up her phone from the table, Nick tapped his to turn it on, and Felix removed his from his pocket.

I, on the other hand, grabbed a trusty notebook of paper, and we got down to business. I ran them through the things Goldy and Pops had brought up, including the soon-to-be marriage, the fact that Leo had a lot going for him, and Janina's moonlighting.

I also added in the part about the tire tracks on Leo and the suicide note that seemed convenient, not to mention the fact that he'd killed himself at the golf course. Why? Because it would be more public? It was a possibility, of course. Maybe. I also threw the family feud in for good measure. And the fact that I had no idea what the suicide note had said.

When I was done they all stared at me as if I'd grown another head.

"What?" I touched my hair just to make sure that the new pixie cut I'd had done at the salon didn't have cowlicks making it stick up in awkward places.

"I'm impressed, sister of mine. I don't think I would have

gotten that much to work with in the last four hours if I'd tried, which I did. It's like you're a magnet for information. All I found out is that Leo had done a stint in a rehab center and was making progress toward staying clean."

"Yeah, where did this all come from?" Maribel used her finger to turn the list toward herself as I slid into a chair at the table after giving what felt like one of those dreaded book reports from third grade.

I loved to read, but I hated to take the book apart and analyze it. And yet that was exactly what I was setting myself up for with all this missing information, just in reverse. Gather everything and then analyze. I'd rather read the finished product, but that wasn't going to happen at the rate the police were moving, unless Maribel had something to add.

I looked in her direction, and she glanced down at her phone again.

"I don't have even a tenth of what you have," she said. "And I'm pretty sure I have everything the police have. I put a call in to dispatch, and they weren't hearing much chatter and think that it really is being handled as a suicide. The coroner can't get here from the mainland for a couple of days so they're putting Leo on ice at the morgue for the foreseeable future."

"That's the same thing I heard," Felix agreed.

"And I just got here, so I'm just getting clued in to what's been going on beyond Leo's rehab." Nick shrugged again, and I couldn't help but laugh.

"So, am I like the team leader or something? I hand out assignments, then we all report back with what we find out when we find it?" I had just wanted to run my own little shop on a quiet little island, yet now I was like the chief of the Island Amateur Sleuth Hour. What on earth had brought me to this? Oh right, my own curiosity and being afraid that justice wouldn't get done. Sigh.

"Works for me," Maribel said and the two men nodded in agreement.

"Fine, but don't let this take up too much of your time. I really am just going to ask around and hand over anything I find to the police. There's no need for us to get more involved than that. They can't make a decision on how he died until the coroner sees him anyway, so we have a few days before it gets marked permanently as a suicide."

We talked for a few more minutes until I happened to glance at the clock and realized it was heading toward ten. I had to get up early tomorrow and face Goldy and her arriving shipment. I knew I could handle it, but on top of everything else the thought was wearing me out.

Tomorrow was a new day, though, and I sank against the doorframe after I escorted the guys out to the front sidewalk. "Let me know what you find out," I said as I closed the door behind them.

I turned and found Maribel looking at me out of squinty eyes and Whiskers mimicking her expression.

"What?"

"Don't even give me the slopey shoulders and taxed face. You know you want to know what happened as much as I do. You also know we're not going to find out if we don't do something." She tapped her lip with just a fingertip. "Maybe I should think about going into private investigating instead of this cop thing. I wonder what it would take to hang out a shingle."

"I don't know that you'd have a lot to do here on the island as a private investigator."

"Yeah, and you didn't think I'd have a lot to do as a police dispatcher either . . ." She raised an eyebrow and then winked at me.

"As much as this seems like an episode of *NCIS* sometimes, I really feel like this one will be important." I pulled my notebook to me as I sat back down at the kitchen table. "Depending on whom Leo's beneficiary is—that is, if he had an insurance policy—there's sometimes a clause that they don't pay out if suicide is involved. And we have all these questions but no answers." I slunk down in my chair and Maribel sat across from me.

"I really do think that the police will take this one seriously—at least I hope so—and we've about talked ourselves out on this one for the moment." She rose from her chair and tapped the table. "Why don't we head to our beds and reconvene tomorrow? This will all still be here."

"No doubt, unless they find the killer overnight." It could happen. In fact, I'd love it, if only to let me off the hook.

"There's always that hope." She brushed a hand over Whiskers' back. "Sleep well, Whit. I'm sure everything will look clearer in the morning. Then you can run out to get all those answers you crave like a Butterfinger."

I laughed as she meant me to, but I also had a lot on my mind. And right now the first thing was making sure that all my ducks were in a row, and I had a plan of attack. Going in willy-nilly was not my style. Not that I really *had* a style when it came to sleuthing.

This was only my second time trying to figure things out, and I really hoped I didn't get in as far as I had last time. I was no Velma in the Scooby-Doo gang, and I certainly wasn't going to try to make sure I could hand the culprit in by the scruff of his or her neck. Staying out and staying safe were the name of the game this time. That and keeping my sanity intact.

Chapter 7

About midmorning the next day, I could have laughed if I didn't feel so much like crying. The early morning had been smooth enough. Whiskers did her things and scarfed down all the food I put in her dish, then looked at me accusingly when I didn't open another can. She had a much smaller area to roam now than she had in Long Beach and had taken to mostly lying in the sun patch from the front window.

With her lack of activity, she was getting chubby, which I thought might be a problem. Not that I'd tell her that since she'd probably do something vindictive like knock over my favorite seashell lamp. But she *was* getting chubby, and the few times Maribel and I had both accidentally fed her in the morning had spoiled her. Now I had to get her back on track, knowing it wasn't going to be pretty but had to be done.

But back to the crying. I'd had no less than thirty people come in to the store. This would have been fantastic if it hadn't only been those looking for information or snooping around. Not a single person bought anything, and I was still dreading that delivery from Goldy.

She'd sent me a text a few minutes ago to let me know her tracking system said an hour until delivery. I didn't always believe those things, but on an island this small the delivery people usually knew what they were talking about.

In the meantime, I busied myself with straightening things here and there and checking my phone to see if any of the people I had wanted to talk to had called me back.

Not a single one. Crap! Even Betty hadn't called back, and I was hoping she could at least tell me what the feud was about. I had a really hard time believing that no one seemed to remember how it started, yet it was still roiling like it had happened last week.

I was composing another text to her to see if I couldn't scare her into answering me when Jake Ahern came strolling into the Dame of the Sea like he might be contemplating owning the place.

"Can I help you find something?" I asked as he sauntered over to the counter in the back, looking and touching things. People did that all the time, it was obviously part of the whole owning-a-trinket-store thing, and yet right now I wanted to smack his hand and get him to move away. Like preferably out of my store altogether.

I did not like how he'd handled things yesterday at the murder scene. I wanted to tell him that but I really did not want to start that kind of conversation when it was just the two of us in here.

"You need a hobby, Whit?" He picked up a shell with googly eyes on the rising hump.

"Uh, no."

"Something to do to fill your time, then?" He balanced the shell in his hand and moved his arm straight out from his body and over the floor. Was he going to drop it on the ground so I could clean it up?

"You break it, you buy it," Goldy said from behind him and he almost dropped the shell, even if he'd only been threatening to do that earlier.

But at least I had backup now.

"What do you want, Jake?" Nick said, coming in right behind our grandmother. Double backup. This I could definitely do.

Feeling much more confident, I leaned forward with my palms on the sales counter and looked him right in the eye, waiting to see what else he had to say.

"Just to see what you think you're doing." But it didn't come out quite as strong and aggressive as he had started out when it was just me.

"I don't think that's what you really want," I said.

"You're nosing into things you shouldn't be," he finally said, belligerence shading his voice. "We don't need anything from you. You're just going to clog up the investigations with your questions and your theories."

"I haven't done either at this point. I haven't asked any questions, and I have no theories. But if you have one you'd like to share, I'm all ears." I crossed my arms over my chest and leaned back against the bookcase behind me. Goldy came around the counter to stand next to me in the same stance. Nick chose to stand out by the edge of the counter, only a few steps from the would-be bully.

A second later, I caught movement in my peripheral vision. Jake had not come alone. There were two men standing outside the front door, flanking it like enforcers or bouncers.

I hadn't seen them at first, and I wasn't sure if they'd come after or before Goldy and my brother walked in. I'd have to ask them later. What did Jake think I was going to do? Run? Hit him?

"Look, I don't know what you and your family are doing here but I can tell you that you're not going to intimidate me."

One of the men turned in to the store with a frown. "We're not trying to intimidate you. We're trying to make sure you don't waste your time." He came fully into the store and I now saw it was Fred Ahern, with a big smile on his face and his hands spread before him. That was a quick change and it felt faker than the starfish the convenience store on the island tried to sell you with a twenty-ounce drink.

"Sorry about Jake," Fred said with a jovial laugh. "I thought he'd be better at this since he's supposed to be a park ranger. You'd think he'd have better people skills." He slapped his nephew upside the back of his head. "Go back to your job. You're not needed here."

Jake pouted and set the shell down harder than necessary, then stalked out of the shop.

Fred shook his head and laughed for a minute. "I really am sorry. I thought that since Jake is your age and a public servant he'd be better at talking with the public, but apparently I was wrong."

I did not trust that smile or the good cop/bad cop scenario. However, I wasn't going to say anything right now just to see what hand they thought they were holding before I sent him off behind his nephew.

"No harm done." Goldy nudged me.

"Sure, no harm. What can we do for you?"

Nick continued to stand at the edge of the counter, like a guard dog that could get to the man before he could touch me, if Fred even tried. I appreciated my brother more than I could say.

"Nothing, really. I'm here to do something for you, though. I don't want you to waste any more of your time looking into poor Leo's death. I promise you that it was a suicide so you don't have to keep trying to find things out around town. It's all very sad but true. We even have a suicide note to prove it." He patted the pocket of his shirt.

That was a whole lot of words that just said the same thing over and over again. And to say I didn't trust him was a complete and utter understatement. The police station would still have the suicide note as evidence and there was no way they would have given it to Fred. Why would they, being that he was on the other side of the family feud?

I decided to go for diplomacy, though, just to get him and his relatives out of my store.

"Thank you." I wanted to lean on the counter and get in his face; instead I tightened my crossed arms and waited for him to leave.

But he continued to stand in the store with his knee-length shorts and his plaid short-sleeved shirt open over a white T-shirt. He squinted at me. Maybe to see if I was going to say anything else? I wasn't. I'd just wait him out at this point. At least I had Goldy and Nick by my side. I wouldn't have wanted to do this confrontation with three on one. Goldy alone would have put us over the top, but having Nick here calmed my fears more than I would have thought.

"That's all you have to say?"

I nodded so as not to say anything else.

"So you're going to stop looking into this?" he pressed.

"I'll take that into consideration." That was the last thing I was going to give him.

"I want your promise." His lips flattened and his hands fisted at his side.

"You're not going to get it, Fred, so back off. She heard what you said and she told you that she'll think about it. That's all. Now leave." Nick took one menacing step forward.

And even though I didn't know what to do with my hands, Goldy certainly knew what to do with hers as she waved Fred out of the store like she was shooing a fly out of her face. "Get going. I know your hearing aids are working since Bernie down at the pharmacy helped you find new batteries just the other day. Scat."

Also so many ways of saying the same thing, but Goldy's were far more pointed and worked better. Fred harrumphed, turned toward the door, and took his nephew and his son with him as they trounced away down the bricked sidewalk out front.

"Phew." I leaned back against the bookcase behind me and fought the urge to wipe my brow. Not that I was sweaty. I was just extremely happy to have that over with.

"If you think it's over you are sadly mistaken," Goldy said. "I guarantee you they'll be constantly in your business the second you step out of this store, and wanting to know who you talk to and what they say." Goldy bustled around the store, straightening things that were already straightened, and I guess working off the nervous energy that seemed to have bounced off that whole encounter.

Nick and I both watched her flit like a butterfly and shared a look. It was better to let her run out of energy before engaging her again.

But I couldn't help myself from interjecting, "Maybe I shouldn't do this." I bit my pinky fingernail, something I hadn't done in a long time.

Last time, I had looked into a suspicious death because my brother's freedom was on the line. That had made sense, and I'd do it all over again to make sure he wasn't wrongly accused.

But this time it was more like being curious. Of course I wanted justice too, but who was I to say that the police wouldn't be able to make that justice happen and probably a lot better than I ever could?

"Don't you even think about it," Goldy said. "Now more than ever you have to do the right thing and ask all the right questions, no matter how uncomfortable it might make people. No matter the secrets that might get uncovered. Do you know who else Fred is related to?" She stood before me like a warrior goddess.

"I don't, but that brings up a great point. Why do I have to be the amateur sleuth, and drag Maribel, Nick, and Felix along with me, when you're the one who has far more access to everyone than I do? You could call up any number of people on this island and make them talk with you through friendship. Heck, you could just use intimidation. I'm the little fish in the big huge sea while you're the whale in the puddle." I threw my hands in the air and then slapped them down on the outsides of my thighs. That hurt but I didn't even wince, just kept constant eye contact with the woman who always seemed to want to push me past my breaking point.

Nick snorted to my right, and I resisted looking at him to see what he thought was so funny.

"Did you just . . ." Goldy swallowed hard with her hand on her throat. "Did you just call me a whale?"

Oh no. I gulped myself and waited for the scathing words to come boiling out of her mouth. No wonder Nick was snorting. My God.

Because an angry Goldy could be far more dangerous, especially if I insulted her. Like the time I'd told her in no uncertain terms that she was going to be Grandma not Goldy and she'd just have to live with it. I was pretty sure she boiled a few fish right out of the sea with her tirade in response.

So I was totally taken off guard when she guffawed like a hyena that'd just been told a bawdy joke around the watering hole.

"A whale—oh, that's rich. I can't wait to tell your grandfather that you called me a whale. He's going to have a field day with that one."

I didn't think it was that funny. I even elbowed Nick to get him to stop snickering. And I certainly did not want her telling Pops about it because he could very easily be mortified that I'd disrespected my grandmother like that.

"That was a poor choice of words. I'm sorry. I was simply talking about being a big fish in a small pond and used the wrong animal." Time for damage control.

"Oh no, don't back down now, sweetheart." She slung an arm over my shoulder and the other over Nick's. "Go for it, say what's on your mind, and don't hold back. A whale." She chuckled. "I have to text your grandfather."

I took her phone out of her hand. "It's not that funny, Goldy, and I didn't mean it like you were big or anything." Was I just digging myself a deeper hole? I thought that might be the case when she laughed her big laugh again. I'd be to the center of the Earth in a few more words at this rate.

"No, no, no, I should have explained before." She took her phone back and put it in her pocket. "Thomas, that dear husband of mine, was just saying that sometimes I bounce around like a whale in other people's lives. It's as if I don't even realize that they might need room to make their own decisions too, because I'm taking on everything myself."

Wow, I wasn't even sure I wanted to touch that with a forty-foot fishing trawler. "Um." Yeah, that was the best I could do under the circumstances. Nick wasn't any help at all as his snickering had turned into complete silence. Traitor. I'd get him later for that.

"No need to respond. I just think he'll get a kick out of it, being that he's going to think he's right, and that I need to back off from trying to 'help,' as I call it—or 'interfere,' as he calls it." She took her phone back out, then typed something in before returning it to her pocket. "So in keeping with that thought, I'll tell you that you can do whatever you feel is right. And the reason I don't step in is that I can't be as clandestine as you are. Everyone knows me and tells me what they want me to hear. They seem to tell you things they never would tell me. Plus, you can move around behind the scenes in a way I've never been able to do. Take that as you will."

I didn't know what to say for like the fifth time in as many minutes so I shook my head. Fortunately, the door swung open at that point and Sam, the delivery guy for the post office on the island, came in with a set of towering boxes on his dolly. Goldy squealed and clapped her hands.

Maybe I should have said *un*fortunately.

Chapter 8

Nick took delivery of the boxes and set them on the floor.

"Why didn't you have me pick these up from the mainland?" he asked Goldy as he checked out the address labels.

"I wanted to make sure they were delivered as soon as possible. You aren't always the most reliable of deliverymen when it comes to my stuff. Other people, absolutely, and they rave about you. But when it comes to me, you sometimes forget to be timely."

She threw him an arched eyebrow as he sulked and then smiled devilishly. "Touché."

"Exactly." But she smiled back at him before returning to my question. "I'm telling you this is going to be just what the shop needs to get on its feet and off to a running start."

"I thought I was already doing a pretty good job," I mumbled. Not soft enough for her to miss it, though.

She slung that arm back around my shoulders and pulled my head down to kiss my crown. If she gave me a noogie I was running.

"You're doing a marvelous job, but a little new stuff here or there isn't going to hurt your business. As I said earlier I plan on these being on consignment, which means no financial risk for you." She turned in a slow circle, doing a three-sixty of the shop. "Now where should I put these?"

She obviously wasn't asking for my opinion or my permission. "I'll be in the back with my laptop if you need me."

She barely nodded in my direction as Nick handed her a box cutter and they got down to the business of cracking open the tape holding the boxes closed.

I knew that no matter what I said she would probably agree in her blissful state. But I didn't test the limits of that. I had a few things I wanted to look up on the internet, and Goldy could handle the front of the shop with Nick while I was gone and they were unpacking.

Besides, I really would rather be surprised, even though I didn't like surprises. But I was weighing trying to hide my facial expressions for the entire time she would unload her new merchandise against just having to do it once with her in my view. I chose the latter.

Where the front of my store was busy with knickknacks and doodads, the back was almost monkish. I had a few shelves, neatly arranged with shopping bags, several rolls of tape, and neatly stacked boxes for shipping. Other than that the place was bare, the desk empty of all things except one small jar of pens. I didn't mind the chaos at all out front, since it was organized chaos. But in here I liked things neat and minimal. I didn't have that at home, I didn't have it out front, I didn't have it in my head, so at least here I could keep it pristine.

Sitting at the desk, I pulled up the internet and then just hovered my fingers over the keyboard for a few moments. How did I even want to go about this? What keywords could I put in to bring up information on either family? It wasn't like they were famous in any way, so there wouldn't be articles on them in national papers. At least I didn't think so. But it was worth a try.

I typed in *Ahern* and got asked if I meant Armani and a list of things involving the country of Armenia. I went through all the arrows at the bottom looking for something more, but when I hit page ten I gave up and drummed my fingers on the desk. What else could I put in that would narrow things down?

I tried *Ahern Catalina* and that at least cut down the chatter. But this was going to take forever. It might be better to just go out and do that talking Goldy thought I did so well.

I was stuck in here for the moment, though, unless I wanted to walk out while she was reorganizing my store.

So I sat back in my chair and dialed Maribel. Maybe she'd have something to shed some light on what I might need to know.

"Oh my, were you reading my mind? I was going to call you on my lunch, but was dying to contact you now. You will never believe what's going on, and I have to tell someone or I'm going to burst like a freaking bubble!"

After she stopped talking, I rapidly clicked a pen I'd grabbed from the jar a dozen times, waiting for her to say something more. "Spill, then."

"Seriously, a bubble. It's like my mind is blown, and if I don't share it with someone soon I might just tumble right out of my desk chair, and this thing has arms."

I sighed and waited for her to peter out, clicking my pen some more. This would be my exercise for the day.

If I tried to force her to stop babbling and get to the point, it could take twice as long as she apologized for talking too much.

So I waited. And I waited some more. Then she finally took a breath, and I broke in. "Maribel, seriously. Please just tell me what you found out. I've never had so many people talk around a point in one day. It's like a disease today. What the heck?"

That at least got her to laugh. "I don't think we need any more diseases around here, right? So we're having a knock-down-drag-out fight between two factions of the sheriff's station. We've got one set who refuses to believe that it was suicide and another that refuses to believe it's anything but, and Fred Ahern was just down here with some kind of note that he swears is a strong claim for suicide. He's going to take it to the mayor—his brother, by the way—if we don't stop doing anything but acknowledge that the man killed himself and leave it at that."

"What side is Captain Warrington on?" I winced when I asked because I was pretty sure I knew.

"Well, since we just got an email instructing that no one is allowed to look at this as anything but a suicide, I'm pretty sure he's siding with the Aherns."

"But—"

"No buts. We have officially ruled it a suicide, and the captain is confident that the coroner will sign off on it as soon as he gets to the island at the end of the week. I think he's getting pressure from the mayor."

"Oh great, I'm going against the mayor and now I have a definite deadline." I winced at the callousness of my remark, but Maribel skated right over me.

"Well, at least you know what you're working against. You *are* working, right?"

"Pfft, I guess I am now. I need some keywords to look up things that the two families might have against one another. No one seems to know what this feud is about. They know it's there but not why, and feelings are strong about the whole thing to the point where no one is taking a step back and wanting the truth unless it fits their agenda."

"I know you might not want to do this, Whit, but I really think you'll have a lot better luck out on the street instead of on the computer."

I winced again because I knew she was right. But I didn't want to cross swords or words with the Ahern family. Not that I was scared. I just didn't want the conflict. But this was important.

"Okay, I'm making a list of the people I want to talk to and the things I need to know. If you think of anything we'll talk about it tonight. Will you have time to have dinner?"

"I should be done at eight. Is that going to be too late?" she answered.

"We'll make it snacks, instead, and depending on what Goldy is unpacking out front I might not want to work here anymore come morning."

"Oh, it's not going to be that bad. Your grandmother has wonderful taste. Maybe a little over the top sometimes, but still wonderful. She knows what she's doing."

"From your lips to the universe's ears." We said goodbye and I braced myself to go back out to the store. It couldn't be that bad. Goldy did know what she was doing in many things, and her sense of style, while a little over the top, still fit her to a T. She'd probably bought something that would literally soar off the shelves and outshine every other thing I'd tried to sell.

Feeling much better with the attitude adjustment, I stood up from the desk, smoothed down my shirt, checked to make sure my shoes were tied despite the fact I was currently wearing slip-ons, and then sighed. Hiding here was not going to make this better.

"Goldy?" I said as I cracked the door to the back room open and peeked out.

I said her name again when she didn't answer. And again as I came out of the back room and ran out to the street. No one better have hurt her. Had Fred and his goons come back and hurt my grandmother because we hadn't given them the answers they wanted?

I would take them apart with my bare hands.

I would call Pops and he'd take a hammer to them. When someone touched my shoulder from behind, I whipped around with my fists raised.

"Can we at least talk about the display before you take me

out with your kung fu fists?" Goldy smiled at me as if nothing was wrong.

I fell on her with a hug that she probably hadn't had since I was five and trying to get her to pick me up.

She might have to pick me up this time too.

"I was so scared!"

"What the heck is going on?" She ran her hand over my hair and then cupped my chin. "What on earth is wrong with you? Did something happen? Who do I have to punch? I'm ready. Oh, I'm so ready."

I started laughing because I just couldn't help myself. I had a feeling that we were both on edge after that little visit earlier and both trying to hide it behind other things.

"Where's Nick?" I said.

"He thought he might be more helpful looking around at the other shops instead of standing here. He got irritated when I wouldn't let him help with the display, so I sent him on his way."

"I love you so much, Goldy."

"I love you too, sweetie." She pinched my chin. "I take it we're not fighting anyone?"

"No, I thought I was going to have to come out swinging when you didn't answer and I didn't see you. Where were you?"

"Taking pictures." She shrugged. "I was going to text them to you so you had time to process before seeing it in person."

"Should I be scared?"

She laughed, the little devil, and grabbed my arm. "It's really not that bad, and whatever you think I have planned is probably nothing compared to what it actually is."

I closed my eyes because I wasn't ready yet. She stood me in front of what I figured was the back corner of my shop. The place wasn't that big to begin with, which made it easier to gauge where exactly she had me walk.

Rent on the island wasn't cheap. I'd done numerous calculations to see what I'd have to bring in every month and what would go out at the same time to make sure I wasn't going to drown. Dedicating a piece of the back wall to something that Goldy was obviously so excited about wasn't going to hurt me. Right? Right.

"Open your eyes, silly. You'd think I wanted to carry those old yard decorations with just the rear end and legs of the person showing."

I remembered those. It looked like someone was bending over from the waist to garden and it was just a big huge fanny on display for the whole world to see. Usually in bright red polka dot pants. I hadn't even thought of those in years. Thank goodness I hadn't, or I might have been even more of a mess than I currently was.

At this point I was making it worse for myself than just opening my freaking eyes and gathering my wits about me. I could do this.

Still, I only cracked open my eyes just the barest bit and tried to see through my lashes.

"I swear to you, I'm going to hold your eyelids open with toothpicks if you don't knock it off." She elbowed me, and I sighed.

"Fine."

"Oh my gosh, aren't those the cutest things ever! Aren't they the ones you buy and put all over the island for other people to find? Are you going to have a paint station for people to paint their own, too?"

My eyes snapped open to zero in on Maribel and then I shot my gaze over to the display. Rocks. Tons and tons of rocks on the shelf in baskets, in little cradles, standing on shelves. And they were all painted with witty sayings and adorable pictures.

"What did you say you do with them?" I asked.

Goldy took one from its display and held it in her hand like she would a baby chick. She showed it to me as if it were a prized possession, and I guessed that wasn't too far off the mark from the wonder on her face. "Rocks, painted rocks to be exact. People buy them here and then they can leave them on the trails for other people to find. I saw it on social media and thought what an amazing thing to find out on a walk. You're strolling along, taking in the sea air, pumping those arms and legs, and suddenly you're stopped by the sight of this adorable little guy."

I couldn't deny that he was adorable. It was a smaller rock with a teddy bear holding the sun in his cupped hands above his head and smiling at it.

"I just love these things." Maribel took another rock from the display. "I want to buy three, and I don't even care what they cost. I could put them down when I go out and then hopefully I'll find other ones." She turned to me. "The point then is to either take it home if it really speaks to you or move it to another location for someone else to find. Most people move them instead of keeping them. I especially like the ones with the sayings on them."

I gave myself time to really look at each rock and they were beautiful—from funny to chic to cartoons and real works of art. I could feel myself smiling. And they'd be out around the island for people to enjoy and maybe want to buy their own to place during their vacation. Or take home with them as a souvenir.

"I am so glad it's not a bunch of feather boas," I said before I could stop myself.

"Really? Feather boas? You must think I lack any kind of class. Let's add that to being a whale," Goldy said, but she did scoot over a little bit and kind of spread herself along the rack next to the rocks.

Had she gotten more than just rocks? "Just let me see it already." I closed my eyes again for a moment and when I opened them I was delighted. Scarves. "They're beautiful." I let a few with watercolor prints run through my fingers and enjoyed the way the soft, silky material floated over my hand and slid between my fingers. "Where did you get all this?"

"Well, I have a friend on the mainland who does a lot of art and was recently laid off from her day job. I thought it might be interesting to see how well her stuff would sell out here while she's looking for another job."

Goldy, the ultimate caretaker, though she could be abrupt and heavy-handed about it. No matter how she went about it, she always seemed to mean well, and these two things were amazing additions to my shop's collection.

"Do you have prices?"

She took a sheet off the first shelf. "They're all right here. Most of these have been sitting around her house for years, so she's not too worried about profit, except that it would be nice to be able to make more if this works out. She has a line on a few jobs already, and as a former CEO I don't think she'll have a tough time getting something soon. In the meantime, this helps her not have to run her shop online. I told her we could ask people to take pictures along their walks, then post them to websites with hashtags of her name and the store's name to garner more tourists."

"Always thinking," Maribel said and bumped up against my shoulder. "Goldy is something else."

"What, I haven't quite figured out yet, but you're completely right. I should have trusted you, Goldy. I'm sorry."

"Pshh, I wouldn't have trusted me either, and if you don't think for a second that I didn't consider those gardening rear ends, then you're kidding yourself. But how would people get them back to the mainland? And most people around here don't have gardens. Although they're not completely off the table since I had asked one company if they would be able to make them into mermaids. They're currently researching the possibility."

My head was spinning with all the information she was laying down. But it occurred to me in the midst of the maelstrom that Maribel was here when she should have been at work. I'd said goodbye to her this morning on my way out the door as she was fighting Whiskers for counter space in the bathroom, and I'd just hung up with her on the phone.

I turned to where she still stood smiling in the doorway. "Maribel, why are you here? Shouldn't you be at your desk doing things?"

The smile dropped and her shoulders sagged. "I was, but then I heard that the coroner is coming Friday instead of next week, and I thought I should warn you in person, so that we could get a game plan together. We have two days, Whit. This is going to remain a suicide if we don't have something to offer as an alternative with concrete evidence behind it, not just suppositions."

Well, that wasn't exactly what I wanted to hear, especially when I hadn't found a single thing to point to that alternative—unless you counted my own unease and my grandfather's gut.

Chapter 9

A plan. A plan was what we needed, and yet I had a ton of ways I could go, but no definite path to get there. And I definitely had no idea which one would get us what we needed to save Leo's reputation, since we couldn't save him.

"Okay, so start getting some intel if possible. Are you still going to search around the office?" I asked Maribel.

"I can, but really everything that doesn't lead to suicide is being sidelined, and I have class tonight. That's why I'm out until eight."

"I'll help." Goldy turned from her rock display with her hands on her hips. "I know I said I wouldn't, but the timeline just got moved up. Nick is out there too. We can't let Leo's murder go unpunished. I want whoever did this to him to pay, not have a get-out-of-jail-free card just because some idiot in the station decided not to look further than his loyalties. I'll go do my whale impression, and we'll see what I can blow out. Starting with the fact that Leo never went near the golf course because he thought it was a game for preppies, not his thing."

She whisked out the door, trailing her purple chiffon scarf behind her. Maribel and I looked at each other in silence. I was the first to break it.

"I think I'm in over my head. It was one thing to try to save my brother from being wrongly accused, but this is a whole new game. I don't think I'm up to it. Where do we even start?"

"We've already started, Whit. Don't lose steam now. We just have to dig deeper and faster." She bit her lip and tapped her finger on her chin. "Where's Felix today?"

"Diving lessons."

"Has anyone been shopping today?"

Looking around at my crowded shelves and knowing that my till was in no way changed since I'd put it in the cash register drawer told the story. "The answer to that is no. I had three goons come in earlier, but other than that no one is buying anything." I explained about the Aherns—Fred and Jake and Fred's son—standing outside my door and threatening me to lay off the investigation.

"Fred's been busy today, then. I guarantee you any note they have is a complete fake." Maribel paced in front of Goldy's new display, which really was pretty on the wall. I could just imagine all those rocks going out into the world and making people smile. I needed a smile just now too, but we had more important things to do.

"So it didn't go through the police department?" I asked, remembering that Jake had said that the paper I had seen pinned on Leo Franklin's coat at the scene was a suicide note.

"No, and that surprises me. I mean, since they're related to each other and the chief seems to want to make this a suicide, I would think the note would have been brought in right away. Did you see it?"

"No, but the issue goes beyond that," I said. "The note was at the actual crime scene. The thing was pinned to the victim's jacket, for heaven's sake. Jake was the one who pointed it out at the golf course in the first place. He told me it was all a nice little package, essentially. But then why did Fred pat his breast pocket like it was there? As he did, he told me to trust him enough to get out of the game." He hadn't been overly forceful in his words, or his actions for that matter, but beneath the smile was a definite demand to listen to him and follow along with what he wanted, just because it was what he wanted.

I didn't work well with those kinds of demands. Even if I had truly believed Leo had killed himself, I probably still would have been moved to look into things because of being told not to. It was a flaw in my makeup, but it wasn't the worst thing a person would have to deal with in life.

"I would have really liked to see the note." Maribel picked up rocks and put them down. No smile on her face this time.

"Me too. But I doubt he'd hand it over, even if we asked nicely."

"Yeah, no doubt. And if he hands it in to the station it'll probably never come close to my desk. But I'm taking an elective right now about handwriting analysis, and I might have been able to tell if it was real."

"Unless they printed it off a computer."

"But if they printed it off a computer then we could see whose computer it was. I highly doubt any Ahern had access to Leo's laptop, dead or not."

She bit her lip again and I bit mine. "Should we see if your date from the other night could get us an in on the family?" I hadn't wanted to ask, and when she turned to me with her eyes narrowed, I knew I should have stuck with my first instinct.

"So now you want me to play nice with Fabian Halston, the guy that you thought was all wrong from the beginning?"

I lifted my hands in surrender. "Forget I mentioned it. Sorry. I am just trying to think outside the box and come up with some way of at least getting some concrete evidence to start with. It's like there are all these ways things could go but I don't know how to get them started."

Blowing out a breath, she came to stand next to me. "I know, I know, and now that I'm thinking about it, it's not such a bad idea after all. I could see if he's available for dinner, I guess, before my class."

I hugged her. "Do that. I think I'll run over to the *Catalina Islander* and see if they have any old newspaper articles that I can read through. The internet is probably not really going to help this time unless I can get specific people to look up. Anything else might be too long ago to have been scanned in or posted online."

Her decisive nod told me she was totally on board. "All right, then, we have our missions, and I would think Felix will be able to do some poking around when he's done with his lessons. You said Nick was out in the shops so all our bases appear to be covered. Especially with Goldy also out there nosing around." She went to the door and opened it. "We've got a deadline. Let's get on it before it runs out."

And with that she was gone with the soft ocean breeze that was coming in off Avalon Bay.

We lived in a small community. Or at least it was a small community that lived here. The rest of the people were tourists. And it wasn't like some random person could have killed Leo for no apparent reason other than that they were psychotic, but I wasn't a big believer in coincidences, and that one would have been huge. Not to mention the way he'd been run over by a vehicle, either during or after his death.

Speaking of which, I needed to see if I could talk with Manny and Aaron Franklin. I'd left messages on their phones, but neither of them had gotten back to me.

Aaron was probably the first one to see his nephew Leo, and he might have run him over by accident. Plus, Manny had been on his way to see Aaron and that rare bird Manny wanted for his book of sightings, and he was talking to Aaron when I found them.

If Aaron had told Manny on the phone that he'd found a dead body, I doubt Manny would have left it out when he stalked

out of the store, ranting his irritation about the bird. But I couldn't
rule anything out just yet. I had to keep my eyes open and not
get set on any particular path like the police were. I had to be
open to the possibilities. Though the possibility of it being
Aaron was breaking my heart.

He could be a pain, but that didn't make him a killer. And no
matter how much he loved bird-watching, I just couldn't imagine he'd be distracted enough by it to actually kill someone. Beyond that, he and Leo were related. Wouldn't Aaron have been
the first one to call the police if it had been an accident? Not to
mention that Jake Ahern and his whole family seemed to think it
had something to do with the feud. If that were true then where
would Aaron killing Leo fit in? Unless he'd done it because Leo
was dating someone from the other side?

Checking the sidewalk outside the store, I saw so many people on the move, although no one was stopping in now. Not even
new people to talk about Leo's death. I didn't know why, and I
didn't have time to figure that out.

It would all even out eventually. And with the rocks in place,
there was every possibility I could have a sale to get things moving, or plant some of my own rocks and have people delight in
them, then want to get their own. But since that wasn't happening at the moment, this was the perfect time to head over to the
newspaper office to see what I could dig up. I'd call it a break,
turn the sign on the door to closed, and be back probably before
anyone stopped in anyway.

Because it was a lovely summer day outside I decided to
leave my cart in the alley and walk the few blocks to the office of
the *Catalina Islander*. I enjoyed the way the breeze lightly ruffled my hair, and the sights and sounds of the bustling streets.
The trees stood tall in the breeze and the vibrant colors of the
buildings brought me joy. Not to mention the sea was a lovely
blue against the sandy beach. I absolutely loved living here, trouble or not.

I arrived at the newspaper office to find Reese McLain sitting right at the front desk with a huge smile on her face and a greeting just as I opened the door.

"Hello, Whit, what can we do for you today? Or were you finally going to write us an article on your store and the fun to be had when collecting historical books about the area?"

Now I remembered why I hadn't come down this way in a while. They wanted me to write for them. Because I didn't use my degree often, I had thought it might be fun to write for the paper that went out to about six thousand people every Friday. But then when I actually had to come up with content, it didn't happen.

"Still working on that," I said stiffly. "I'll get it to you."

"Whenever works for you." The smile stayed on her face, but it looked more like sympathy than greeting now.

"Thanks." I fiddled with a few things on the counter, moving a stapler, straightening a flyer, lining up the business card rack with the back edge. "So, um, I was wondering if I could look in the archives here? I have a few ideas about . . ." And there was my entry! "A few ideas about doing a series of articles on what stores have been in my space over the years and how commerce changes as the years pass. I thought it might be a fun idea and pull some history in."

Of course I'd thought no such thing and normally my attempts to lie or even exaggerate went horribly, but it seemed to be working this time. Hooray!

"That's a wonderful idea! I bet I could get everyone to do one! Or maybe you'd like to do them for everyone? It would be a great way to stay in the paper. We do pay, just in case I hadn't mentioned that before."

Hmm, that might not be a bad side gig until I could get more people to come in to the Dame of the Sea. Part of the problem was that it was hard to advertise when you had no idea who was coming over to the island, and I didn't do a lot of internet sales since people wanted to be here when they picked out a souvenir.

Reese stood up from her desk; I had forgotten how incredibly tall she was. I often thought I was average because everyone around me seemed to be just over five feet, but Reese was far closer to six feet, so I ended up being the really short girl for the first time in a long time.

"If you want to follow me, I'll show you the archives. Are you looking for anything else or just the history of the store you run?"

Her back was to me so I couldn't tell if she really was interested or if she was also trying to figure out if I had ulterior motives. I did not want to tell on myself. How to not do that, though, without getting locked in a room with only one kind of article?

See, this is what always happened when I lied: I either got caught or locked myself into a corner.

"Well . . ." I couldn't come up with anything that would sound convincing. I groaned at myself under my breath. Dang it.

She stopped next to a door with a window in it. As I peeked in I could see shelf after shelf of boxes lining the walls of the room. Most likely they held everything the newspaper had on file. I was pretty confident I could navigate it myself without outing myself. *Smart move there, Whit.* "Just my store." I tried to smile but it felt flat. There were a *lot* of boxes. How was I going to accomplish this at all, much less by myself?

You know what? I thought. I'd do it because it was important, and I had really liked Leo Franklin. He deserved justice instead of being pushed aside because of some family feud that no one seemed able to put a real name to.

Well, I was going to do all I could to figure out what the feud was about and whether or not it had anything to do with Leo's death. I had a mission and when I had a mission there was little that could stop me.

The microfiche and I had a date, as soon as I figured out how to use the freaking machine.

Once Reese settled me into a chair, she showed me briefly how to work the huge machine. I paid attention as best I could but knew it was going to take me fiddling around by myself to actually be able to use the behemoth.

A knob turn here and an adjustment there and finally a flood of words came up in the faded screen. I scrolled first for the history of my store because the article really was a good idea and could lead to more. If it paid well then so much the better.

In my scrolling, I found that at one time my store had been a bakery and the other half of a restaurant. It had also once been an animal clinic. That would explain the dog scent I smelled every once in a while, even though I didn't own a dog or let them in the store. It had also been an apothecary and served a brief stint as a small doctor's clinic. Interesting.

After taking some notes, I twirled my chair around to face the wall of boxes and wondered where to even start. The paper had been around for a while but would it have info on a personal feud between the Aherns and the Franklins?

It seemed strange that no one in the families seemed to know what the feud was even about. Then again I hadn't asked very many of them and really I should have been asking the older ones if they remembered. I put a reminder on my list of things to do, which seemed to be growing exponentially.

Standing at the boxes, I ran my fingers over the fronts to see if I could figure out any kind of system. Was it by date? By subject? By some other parameters that I just couldn't figure out? That last one seemed to be the right answer, since I had no idea of what I was even looking at, and I hadn't paid attention when Reese was pulling the information.

After another half an hour of staring at the boxes I finally gave up and went to find Reese. I hadn't come up with a way to figure out how they were labeled. I'd even gone on my phone to see if there were standard labeling systems for this kind of thing, but had been faced with so many different options it was impossible to choose. So I'd tried each one but none of them had fit.

I found Reese at her desk. "Hey there, I think I'm done and have the info for the article. I was wondering about other articles, though. Like maybe I could do other people's stores, like you'd suggested. How would I go about looking up just that information? I tried to figure out your system, but I couldn't." Honesty and a lie all in the same sentence—I called that a win, especially if it got me what I wanted.

Rocking back in her desk chair, Reese moved her dark brown hair off her shoulder and smiled at me.

I smiled back but uncertainty tainted it because hers wasn't like a welcome, or a *Hey, I'm happy to see you.* It was more like a cat that ate the canary. Had I said something to give away my real purpose? Some amateur sleuth I was.

"Why don't you just tell me what you're really looking for, then maybe I can help you more." She steepled her hands in front of her lips that were still lifted up on the sides.

Glancing at the tropical art behind her desk, the plant on her counter, and the framed papers from over the years, I did everything I could to save myself. "I just did. I'd like to offer to do a series on other people's stores and what they've been over the years. I'm just not sure how to find the information since I wasn't paying attention when you got my box out." That sounded legitimate, at least in my mind.

But Reese laughed.

Okay, then.

"Oh Whit, you're so transparent."

I didn't seem to think so but I was sure she was about to tell me why she did.

"Okay?" It was the best I could come up with.

"Of course it's okay. I appreciate that you're looking into

Leo's death. There's no way he would have killed himself. I'd put money on that family-feud thing finally coming to a head. For a while there we had a ton of the family members leave and things had settled down, but over the last six months most of them have come back, and it just seems to be ramping up again. Especially since Leo and Janina had started seeing each other."

I was almost afraid to ask, but I'd feel stupid if I didn't. "And do you know what said family feud is about? Because no one else seems to have a clue and I really need a clue right about now. Or I'm going to have to hand in my honorary sleuth card."

"Of course I don't." She shook her head and laughed. "Nobody does and it's like the greatest mystery of the island if you've been around long enough." She looked to be my age so I didn't know how long that was supposed to be. I'd never heard about it before Leo's death and the few people I'd talked to hadn't either. But I'd play along if it would get me the access I was looking for. Or at least a direction that wasn't all over the place.

"So where do I start?"

"The archives, of course."

"But wasn't I just there?"

"Well, you were kind of there. I just thought it was so cute that you asked for microfiche and that poor machine never gets any use so I let you use it. But the real information is on the database, which you can find on our intranet."

Ah, so that explained the smile. She'd snowed me by making me use the old machinery until I told her the truth. I'd never been a good liar so it was no surprise that now was no different.

"Fine," I conceded with a sheepish smile. "I need to know about the family feud to see if there's anything in it that would lead to the death of Leo. Both sides have mentioned it, yet no one has a definitive answer as to what happened or even when it happened."

"That's more like it!" She practically leaped out of her chair and walked down the hall toward the back of the building.

I tried to keep up with her long strides and ended up breaking into a jog to do it. With her determination, I did not want to ask her to slow down.

"Come on back, and I'll set you up with the right machinery—but you have to promise to tell me if you find anything out." She opened a door to a room filled with computers. "Promise."

Since I couldn't get past the arm she'd thrown out across the doorway, I made that promise. "You'll be the first to know—after me."

"I'm going to hold you to that."

"I don't doubt it," I said. But she let me through the door and then opened up a bunch of windows on a computer at the back of the room. It had the cushiest chair I'd ever sat in. I wiggled a little just to get it absolutely right and then didn't want to get up. I needed to find one of these for myself.

"Don't even think about taking that chair with you when you leave." She snickered.

"Even if I find the reason for the feud and answer an ages-old mystery here on the island of Catalina?" I stroked the arm of the chair, wondering if it would fit in my backpack if I disassembled it. Of course that was ridiculous, but just for a moment I did think about shoving it out the back door and then picking it up in the alley with my golf cart.

"Even then. Steve would kick my rear end off the airport cliff if his chair was missing when he comes in tomorrow."

"Say no more." Steve was not a guy to be messed with. He'd been some kind of hard-hitting reporter over in Los Angeles back in the day. You'd think living on the island would have been his excuse to only report on sunny things and feel-good pieces, but Steve wasn't built that way.

Goldy had had a few run-ins with the guy over the years when he spun stories in a direction she did not like, and I knew better than to get involved. I was just here to find some information, and then I'd leave the computer behind and the chair with it.

In the meantime, I asked Reese how to navigate the system I had never seen before. Once I'd typed in a few parameters and got good answers, I shooed her out of the room and got down to work.

Chapter 10

This was anything but tedious. There was no turning of knobs, or trying to find a word while the plastic film flew by, or missing something and not being able to remember where you'd found it. This was efficiency at its best, and I loved it.

I typed in search words like they were going out of style. I started with the last names of people I knew were related to the Aherns and the Franklins and came up with a bunch of information. The current commander of the Avalon Sheriff's Station, Captain Warrington, had come by his profession honestly, since it looked like he was part of an unbroken line of police officers almost since the island had been inhabited.

Humphrey Ahern established the latest in a line of private police forces in 1911 as one of three officers to police the small but booming island. People were building houses and setting up stores. Of course, they'd probably originally all known one another and so there hadn't been much policing to do. But once tourists had gotten wind of the wonders to be seen over here, and Airport in the Sky opened in 1946, there was far more to do and law and order to keep.

I read article after article about arrests, unrest, illegal fishing, docking without a permit, golf cart crashes, a few accidental deaths—the name of one unfortunate person, Delilah, stood out to me, for some reason—and theft. But nothing that involved the Aherns when I put in police activity. Interesting. Not a single one of them had ever been arrested? I guess if you grew up in the force you either didn't do bad things or were let off if you were caught.

I moved on to the Franklin family and came up with protests during Prohibition, an election they won for mayor over the Aherns, and a history of award-winning gardens galore. They seemed to place every year for best garden until 1976 when the award was stopped.

So unless the Aherns really thought that they should have won and the Franklins were the ones keeping them from winning by cheating or greasing palms, I couldn't see anything that had to do with a feud. They also had very few—like almost none at all—arrests, until after 1930. I would have thought if the police force hated you that they'd be out looking for any excuse to arrest much earlier than that.

Unless 1930 was when the feud had started . . .

With everyone reminding me of my Shakespeare degree lately, I decided to look into the whole lovers-that-shouldn't-have-been angle, but I saw no marriage announcements or birth announcements that linked the two families.

That in itself was astounding. For the size of our population I was blown away by the fact that none of them had ever married one another, especially a hundred years later.

But that did give me pause that Leo and Janina had been dating. Why were they breaking the tradition? Maybe they wanted to? Maybe they figured the feud was dumb. Maybe they hadn't known about the feud?

I put the question on my list for Janina or Sylvie, Janina's aunt and the owner of La Annaffiare, and went back to the articles on the Franklins. They seemed to be good citizens, touting parades and running a few businesses along through the years, though they hadn't stayed in business for long, and the 1920s seemed to be a time where they had little going on but a lot of money. They used that money to throw huge parties and lavish dinners that were covered by the paper in full front-page articles with pictures.

I took more notes and wondered what all this was going to do for me. I still didn't know what the feud was about, and now I had the full history of both families, but nothing to tie it into a murder. Where did Leo fit in?

Or was I looking in the wrong direction? I still hadn't made time to hunt Manny down and find out what he knew beyond the last phone call with Aaron, nor what had happened when he got to the golf course. Which meant I also had to talk to Aaron and see if he actually had run Leo over, by accident or design. Maybe he was the one who was against the two lovers and killed Leo to keep him from sullying the family name.

I closed up shop, or rather just logged out of the computer and took my notepad of information with me. Stopping by the front desk on my way out, I waited for Reese to hang up the phone before saying goodbye to her.

"I think I have everything I could possibly want, plus some." I waved my notepad at her.

"Anything good?" She folded her hands on her desk and leaned in like I had the secrets of the world within my papers.

Laughing, I shook my head. "Yeah, not really unless you count parties where no mingling was done between families and a list of businesses that went in and out of fashion over the years. Sorry."

"Hey, not a problem. But I still want to be first on that list if you find out what the feud was about. I had a feeling it wasn't just going to be in the archives. I think I would have found it when I interned here. I'm the one who had to put all those articles into the database. It was worth a try, though."

"It was. I have some people to talk to. Maybe someone knows more than they're letting on and will let something slip that will make the connection."

"That's what I like about you, Whit, your optimism and your questioning mind. If that shop ever doesn't work out, I might be able to find something for you to do here."

I could feel heat creeping into my face. I wasn't sure if it was because she so casually thought that I might not be able to keep the shop open, or because long ago I had desperately wanted to do something with words but had fallen back on working for the trainyard instead.

"I'll let you know if I find anything."

"Do that. Or if you really want to be nice to me, you could send your brother along with the information. I wouldn't mind that at all." She gave me a cheeky smile. She obviously had no idea what she would be getting herself into with Nick.

"I'll see what I can do."

"I'll look forward to it and your information."

I saluted her without saying anything more and stepped out onto the sidewalk. The light breeze coming in off the ocean smelled like suntan lotion and brine. I headed toward its source.

There was something so wonderful about living surrounded by the sea. All that time I'd spent on the mainland, I'd rarely had time to ever go to the beach, much less just stand at the shoreline and breathe it in. Not to mention the air quality was a lot different in Long Beach from this little piece of heaven in the Pacific Ocean.

I took another breath and then almost released it in a scream when someone tackled me from behind.

Though I was sure I was going to end up with my face in the sand from the force of the shove, I remained upright with someone's hand wrapped tightly around my bicep. And I didn't even drop my notepad.

After a split second where I congratulated myself about that, I narrowed my eyes to find who thought that manhandling me was a good idea.

And found myself face-to-face with Manny.

"Oh, Whitney, I am so sorry about that. I tripped over the curb in my haste to get to you, and I didn't want to fall with all this equipment. Sorry again. Didn't mean to scare you."

His face was red and what little hair he had on top of his head was in disarray. And he wasn't kidding about all the equipment. He had three sets of binoculars, what looked like some kind of whistle, and a flashlight all hanging around his neck, not to mention the two satchels crisscrossing his torso.

"That's okay, Manny, but can you let go? You're hurting my arm."

"Oh, right, right, sorry about that too. Dang, I am just not with it today."

He was also far stronger than I would have given him credit for. He looked a little frail, but that grip had been monumental.

Maybe he had hurt Leo and then had come into my shop to wait until the body was found by Aaron, who was out birdwatching. That was a favorite spot for twitchers, or so I'd heard. And anything was possible at the moment when I knew nothing for sure.

Another mental note tucked away. Quite honestly it was getting crowded in there. I wanted to write all this down before I forgot anything.

Should I grill him now that I had him in my sights? I felt like it might be a good idea, but he started walking away.

"I thought you had something you needed to tell me?" I said to his retreating back.

He stopped and turned around. "Not tell you but ask you. How are things coming with the death investigation? Aaron needs this closed."

"I wish either of you had called me back when I left you messages, then."

"I'm here now, aren't I?"

I sighed and joined him. "Yes, you are. So what do you know about the death? There were tire marks on Leo's jacket. Did Aaron run over Leo?"

He lifted his shoulders in a shrug. "I have no more info than you do. I showed up and the kid was already on the ground. Aaron was bent on killing himself because he thought he shouldn't live anymore if he'd killed his nephew. But he couldn't have run over Leo because the tire tracks only went in one direction. To put Aaron's cart where it was when I showed up, he'd have had to back up over the kid. I guarantee you he didn't do that."

"Then what happened?"

"I thought that's what you were looking into, Madame Sleuther."

"Yeah, not so much."

"Well, you'd better step it up or you're going to have the Aherns on you for interfering and the Franklins on you for not interfering enough."

"Great."

"Ah, it's not so bad. If I think of anything I'll stop in, but for now you're in this yourself, girl. Better start finding some information to keep the pack off your back."

I'd had enough with the pressure and the non-answers, although at least I did have some new information to put in my notebook.

"I should go," I said instead of continuing this conversation with him. "I have to open the store back up." It was as good an excuse as any until I could organize my thoughts and see if there was anything else I needed from Manny. I shook out my arm to get the blood flowing again.

"Meh, your store's already open. Don't lie to me if you just don't want to talk. Goldy's in there, selling those rock things like they're nuggets of gold. Might try my hand at painting a few birds on them. She said maybe she could take them on consignment." He shrugged, and I groaned silently.

I did not need more inventory, but even more than that I needed to ask him questions, even if I wasn't sure what exactly to ask since I couldn't just come out with *Did you have something to do with Leo's death, and are you and Aaron covering it up?*

But now that I had him here, I really couldn't leave without ferreting out more information from him. How to get him to tell me anything more when I couldn't get started? I'd have to come up with something.

"So, Manny, did you ever end up seeing that bird you wanted to yesterday? Did you and Aaron arrange that ahead of time?"

His eyes narrowed. "You think I'd do that, Whit? I told you we were friends and you think I would help him kill his own nephew, then make it look like a suicide?"

I would have expected menace on his face from the words flowing out of his mouth, but instead there was sadness. He shook his head and turned away from me on his sturdy legs.

Now I was the one grabbing his arm. He shook me off and kept walking.

"Look, Manny, I'm sorry. I didn't really think you'd do anything to Aaron, but I have to check every possibility to cross them off my list. I want to find Leo's killer. Unless you think he really did kill himself?"

He turned back to me with storm clouds on his face. "Leo wouldn't have done that to himself. He had too much to live for and too many things he still wanted to do with his life, not to mention a bunch of money to do them with. Why would he off himself just as he was getting his feet back under him?"

"I have no idea, but unless I can figure this out the police are going to have it declared a suicide, and Leo's killer will get away with murder, literally."

That gave him pause. "Those damn Aherns. Is Barney Warrington in charge of that? I'm surprised he didn't change his name when he was old enough to do it. Always wanted so bad to be named Ahern that he plays lapdog to them at the slightest chance."

"Wait a minute. Barney is that desperate to be acknowledged by them?"

"Hell yes, he is. Through his mother's cousin's stepfather or something like that, he's related, and he hauls that around like it's a prize pheasant. Boy doesn't know what to do with himself if he isn't told how to do it by an Ahern."

"How did I miss that?"

"Well, you haven't been here for a while in a long-term capacity, darling, and things would have been way over your head when you were younger. You need to know the players if you want to continue being the island nosy girl and amateur sleuth all rolled up into one. Not everyone can be Jessica Fletcher."

I smiled as his *Murder, She Wrote* reference, then thought more about what I didn't know, and that Manny could be a good source of info that would allow me to not have to always go through Goldy. As long as I could really trust him. And even if I couldn't, as long as he didn't try to push me into a gully, I should be okay.

"I might have some questions later, but I do need to go see what Goldy is doing at the store before she decides to just take it over from me." I patted his shoulder. "Thanks for the info and for not being mad at me for asking. I really didn't think it was you, but I had to at least find out what you knew." Not that I'd really done that, but I did have a few things to follow up on and that was more than I'd had a few minutes ago.

"To answer your question, no, I didn't see the bird, and I almost didn't make it to the golf course at all because I got waylaid by Sylvie coming out of the clubhouse, and then all hell broke loose."

"What did Sylvie want?" This could be useful and yet another thing to put in my mental bank.

"She wanted to make sure that I was still paying for my granddaughter's Sweet Sixteen in advance. I guess there's some trouble in culinary paradise over there, and she needs the money as soon as possible."

Interesting, but not exactly noteworthy. Sylvie's money troubles weren't my concern.

Unless they were. I stopped in my tracks, but didn't say anything. So the aunt was making sure all deposits were in early, and the niece was moonlighting as something. I wished I had a better in with Janina because I really needed to talk to her and get her side of things.

"Wow, that sucks for Sylvie," I said to keep the conversation rolling until I could come up with a way to ask what I really wanted to know. Had Aaron run over Leo and did Manny know about it? "I thought she did good business over there."

"Oh, I think she brings in plenty of money. It's how much she spends that's more of a problem. I heard she's been doing free rounds of drinks almost every afternoon." He smirked and then laughed. "It wouldn't hurt her to be brought down a rung or two, if you ask me. But I do appreciate her cooking and my granddaughter loves that place, so I at least need her to stay in business long enough to pull that off. I'll get her the money today to get her off my back, though. Actually, I should probably go do that now, and let you get back to your shop."

"I appreciate it. And if you think of anything you'll tell me?" I was going to have to let him go without asking the big question. I didn't want to irritate him before I got more from him. Asking again if Aaron had run over his own nephew when Manny had assured me it was impossible would surely throw me right under the bus. Plus, from everything Manny had said, I highly doubted it was a good question in the first place.

"Of course. Like I said, I know Aaron and he would never have hurt his nephew. He's my friend, and I'm not going to let him go down like that if I can help it. Maybe I can dig something up about that feud. I'll get back to you if I do. I'll stop by the store tomorrow if I find anything."

I nodded and smiled and then thanked him. Funny how twenty-four hours and an unsolved murder can take you from wanting to actively kick someone out of your store to hoping they stopped by as soon as possible.

Chapter 11

I made it back to the store just as Goldy was selling another handful of rocks.

"You place them along the trails and they give people a smile when they're out walking. It's a great way to spread cheer, even when you're not physically there."

"So, I buy it and put it out on the road for someone else to find. Isn't that just giving it away?" The guy at the counter looked skeptical as he turned the rock over and over in his hand. "I mean, I might as well just put a five-dollar bill under a rock and expect someone to pick it up and have a good cup of coffee on me."

Goldy's smile never wavered. "Think of it as spreading joy for a small price. Someone might need just the message on that rock."

"Then why don't they buy it themselves and put it on a shelf or something?" He shook his head as he put the rock on the counter.

The woman with him picked it right up, handed it back to Goldy, and shook her own head. "Ring it up. This idiot wouldn't know sunshine if it blasted him in the eye. And I'll take three more, just because." She turned to the man, who looked like he might be her husband from the matching bands on their left hands. "Give her your credit card, dear, or I will."

He still looked skeptical, but that look was being overtaken by sheepishness. "We're here to have a good time, right, Mary Ellen? Of course we can buy rocks if that's what you want."

I coughed to hide my snicker and to alert Goldy I was on the premises. She just smiled and took the credit card as soon as the man dug it out of his wallet. "Would you like to round up for charity? Today we're supporting the Catalina Casino on the is-land for restorations."

His wife elbowed him when he groaned. "Yes, of course," he answered promptly, and I wondered if it was a new marriage or one as old as the hills. Could have gone either way.

Goldy kept smiling and waved them out of the store, then winked at the woman when she turned around at the door with a smirk. "Have fun placing your rocks, darling," Goldy called out.

"We sure will. We're going on a walk now. I'm sure I'll find places for each of them."

"Good for you." Another wink and they were out the door.

"Smooth," I said, placing my bag on the counter.

"Not exactly smooth, but it made the sale, and the woman will probably come back in here for some bauble to take home with her. It's all about future sales, if you can make it happen. And the casino needs help. People who come here think it's for gambling, but we know better. It never hurts for the biggest gathering place building on the island to have donations. It's the first thing most people see when they're crossing the ocean to our little slice of heaven. William Wrigley, Jr. opened it in 1929 ten years after he bought the island; I'm just trying to keep his legacy alive."

"And get a reluctant husband to spend more money."

"Well, there is that." She straightened up the few flyers for local happenings on the counter and smiled at me.

"Got it."

"You do have it, my dear, and you've made this place lovely. I'm so thrilled you're here now. I know I don't say that often enough, but I think it all the time."

"What do you want that I haven't already given you?" I asked with my eyes squinted. Goldy could be a handful. She could be demanding, and loving, and ranting, and overbearing, but she wasn't often open like this. It usually meant there was some kind of favor she wanted.

"Great-grandchildren would be nice," she said airily. "But since you don't seem to be moving in that direction anytime fast, I just wanted to see if you could take the cruise that your grandfather said he'd do for Nick tonight. The man forgot it was the fiftieth anniversary of our engagement, and he's supposed to take me out to dinner at La Annaffiare. Or at least that's what he'll be doing once I tell him I made reservations."

La Annaffiare. The restaurant Sylvie owned and the one that might be in some financial straits. Well, it would be good to have more business there, and Goldy could rack up a tab like few I had ever seen. "Since when do you celebrate the date of your engagement? This is the first time I've ever heard of it."

She brushed a hand along her collarbone. "We celebrate every year." She fluttered her eyelashes, which put me on high alert.

I had a sneaking suspicion . . .

"Do you, now? And is it always on the same day every year?"

She laughed that lofty laugh, the one that reminded me of a vapid socialite and waved a hand at me. "Of course we don't. It's only when I want something that I figure it's time to celebrate our engagement. Plus, it wasn't anything huge the first time, no grand gesture, or a diver coming out of the ocean with a treasure chest for me, like that young couple did a few months ago. And he can never remember the date, so it's easy enough to convince him it's whatever day I say it is."

"Diabolical. That's what you are."

"Oh, please, tell me you're not just learning that now? It's been this way since you were little."

"No, I think I always knew, but living here as an adult has just made it more apparent."

"Smart cookie. Or at least smarter than Pops."

I highly doubted he hadn't caught on. I figured it had more to do with my grandfather knowing that it paid much better dividends to let Goldy think she had pulled one over on you than to call her on it.

Someday I hoped to have a relationship like that. It sounded weird with all the little games they played with each other, but honestly, I thought it kept things lively. And lively was what kept the marriage rock solid.

That and my grandmother had threatened to kill Pops instead of ever letting him leave her. Yeah, that might have had something to do with it too. Especially since the last time she'd made the threat she'd been holding a flare gun in her hand.

"Yes, I can take the cruise. I don't have any plans tonight other than talking with Maribel. Is the cruise for anyone special?"

"Nope, just a few reservations. Oh, and I'm sure you'll get some last-minute walk-ups. It should be quiet, though, and it can give you time to think your way through what you're going to do next to find Leo's killer."

"I know. I'm trying." Blowing out a breath, I retrieved my notebook from the counter and opened it up. "I have so many thoughts and ideas, but nothing concrete. It's driving me crazy!"

"Any new solid information?" she asked as she put a few more rocks back out on the display.

"How many of those did you buy?"

"A lot and more are coming in. They're doing great. And if they don't get moved too much then I believe you and I could go out and find them to move them around."

I bit my lip because I probably shouldn't say what I was thinking. I did anyway. "You don't think it's going to be a problem with the town council that we're introducing a bunch of new rocks to the area?"

Ever confident, she waved a hand at me. "I already talked to Cynthia at the town hall, Whit. She said it's fine. In fact, she loves the idea. I was even told we could pull rocks from the island if they're small enough and let people paint them. Don't you worry about it, I have all my bases covered. You need to concentrate on this murder thing."

"Yes, ma'am."

She narrowed her eyes at me. "I am not yet old enough to be a ma'am."

"Right." But I giggled and ruined it. Which caused her to narrow her eyes even more. She wasn't going to be able to see if I said anything else I wasn't supposed to. I cleared my throat. "I guess I'll head out and get things ready for tonight then, unless you need me in my own store."

After she scoffed, she must have seen the look on my face. I wasn't entirely kidding when I made the comment.

"Oh, sweetie, I'm not trying to take over." She held my hand in hers and stroked my fingers. "I'm just far more bored with retirement than I thought I would be, and the store is adorable. You've done amazing things with it. All I want is just to be a part of it. I promise not to make it mine anytime soon."

And I believed she really would try not to, but I also knew she had a habit of taking over without even meaning to. I might have to give that some more thought. In fact, I'd make it a priority to keep the upper hand once I found out who'd killed Leo.

Right now, though, I needed to go get ready for a cruise and read over the tour script note cards I'd written out when I'd returned to the island to help me remember what I was supposed to say on the tour. I knew most of it by heart from doing the tours throughout my teenage years, and since I got back, but it never hurt to brush up on the flora and fauna of the sea before heading out on a tour where I was supposed to be the expert.

Making my way back to my house, I remembered that Maribel was on the desk today at the sheriff's station. Maybe I could catch her after I wrote down everything I'd learned in the past few hours. It certainly wouldn't hurt to see if she'd be able to add some more light to the situation before she got home.

I also made a note to check in with Felix. Suddenly I felt like I was leading a band of vigilantes instead of just staying in touch with my friends and my boyfriend. Honestly, who did I think I was, to be diving into something like this when it was none of my business and not something I was trained for in the least?

I pulled up at my house and parked the golf cart. An easy mode of transportation, this thing couldn't go fast but at least it got me where I was going. Though I did miss being able to go over fifteen miles an hour and driving a car with actual sides and doors and a trunk.

Maybe I'd head to the mainland and rent one to cruise the coast or go to the mountains. After this I was sure I deserved some kind of vacation. I put that in the back of my mind to discuss with Felix as I opened the front door to Whiskers's meows.

"Oh, come on, I fed you before I left. You're certainly not going to starve anytime soon. Back up." I made the same shooing motion that Goldy had made earlier today, but it didn't work with this cat. Whiskers was nothing if not persistent. She wound her way through my ankles again and again as I tried to walk to the kitchen, almost making me fall into the couch twice.

Finally, I just picked her up and took her with me the last three steps to the small kitchen in the house Maribel and I shared.

Most real estate on this street was small by necessity and because of cost. Some people used the houses for vacation homes, or rented them out to people who wanted to get the island feel and not stay in a hotel. Our square footage was under a thousand feet and I was eternally grateful that Maribel and I got along so well. I couldn't have afforded the rent on my own and that was one of the points I had brought up when I'd convinced my best friend to move with me across the ocean to this tiny place.

Of course, when we were originally planning on moving here I hadn't thought we'd have so much unrest, but I hadn't promised her the world, and she was really enjoying herself with the police department.

And then there was Felix. I cranked open a can of the wet cat food that Whiskers loved, then emptied it into the ceramic bowl one of my artists had made into a fish with scales and everything. After filling the bowl, I placed it on the floor, then leaned back against the counter.

Felix. I hadn't expected to see him again after I'd left the mainland. We'd only casually dated a few times and it was never anything serious.

Or at least that was what I had thought. Check that, it was what I had talked myself into when he hadn't said anything about my moving out of town without him. But then I'd seen him walking along the shore of Avalon Harbor and had been thrilled that he'd come out this way without me having to beg, yet skeptical if an actual relationship between us would ever really work.

And now he'd given up living on the cutter he owned down at the docks and rented a house a few streets over. He was making a life for himself here too. I hoped he didn't regret it with the murders that had happened around here.

However, it was a whole lot cheaper than Long Beach, and he was having a ball with his diving lessons and scuba certifications.

So that meant I was the only one rolling around in uncertainty.

I'd take it, though, as long as I was on my island and at least attempting to get my life into order.

And to get my life in order I also needed to get my island in order, and that meant finding Leo's killer.

After I took a quick shower and got into my sailing outfit.

Hot water and some new makeup went a long way toward making me feel better about everything. I cleaned up after Whiskers, who was still twirling in and out of my ankles, and made sure all her toys were in the right place and that the catnip was out of reach. Recently, she'd taken to helping herself to the stuff. I'd found her sprawled out on the floor in the zone half in and half out of the bag the other day. That couldn't happen again.

Maribel had laughed, but I'd been concerned that the cat might have overdosed, and decided to play it safe by putting the stuff in a cabinet that I blocked with a chair.

That would teach her. Both hers. Or at least I hoped.

Whiskers would probably waste little time finding something else to destroy, I was sure, as that was her modus operandi.

But I knew that when I'd picked her up from the shelter that first day. Within minutes of taking her to my car, she'd decided that the hairband I was wearing was not to her liking and she'd attacked my scrunchy.

Just one more reason why I appreciated my new hairdo. And speaking of that, I made a note to myself to schedule my next haircut. The spa might not have any gossip this time, as I didn't think any of them were related to either side of the feud, but it wouldn't hurt.

While I had the paper out, I finally made myself sit down

and write out everything I knew and all the questions that came along with the things I wished I knew. It was a list that took multiple pages in the end, but it was necessary. I had questions.

Like, how would someone have been able to get Leo out to the golf course? Had he actually killed himself? But with what? I hadn't even heard what had killed him. I made a note to ask.

Or had he been killed? Not exactly the kind of ruminating I wanted to do right before I was supposed to be taking a bunch of happy people out on a glass-bottom boat to enjoy the sea life around our island, but it had to be done. Apparently, I was the one to do it.

I wrote out the info from Manny and my thoughts after my research today on the families at the newspaper's archives. I did wonder how the Franklins had made money when it appeared they had no businesses in the 1920s, but that had to go into the column of questions I needed answers to. That thing was growing by leaps and bounds.

But at least I'd have some direction for tomorrow instead of just wandering around and asking random questions. I had a mission and I was going to finish come hell or . . . well, I was just going to finish it and hope that no high water was in my future, especially as I was due on the boat in thirty minutes.

I slipped my sneakers on, kissed Whiskers on her paw, and then headed back out to my golf cart. It wasn't a long jaunt to the pier, but since I'd be coming home after dark I thought it might be better than walking.

Jumping in, I started it up and then put my bag on the seat next to me. The bottom clunked against something. Something that shouldn't have been there since I'd cleaned the cart out earlier of all debris.

I lifted my bag and found a rock on my front seat. How did that get there? I laughed. Most likely Goldy had put it there for me to hide on my way to the dock for the cruise or something. People would find it and want one of their own and could come in to the store to get it. Actually that wasn't a bad idea. I hoped she had picked a pretty but vibrant one so it stood out against the dark wood of the pier.

I flipped the rock over since the bottom was a natural gray and got the shock of my life. The front had no pretty pictures, no dandelions or tulips. No words of encouragement or wisdom.

No, this rock was black as night with red rivulets running along the surface and the words *Stay the hell out of our business*.

Chapter 12

I put the pedal to the metal as best I could in the little putt-putt and lifted my phone out of my bag at the same time. I had never been so thankful for speed dial and for a vehicle that didn't go fast enough for me to worry.

"Felix, can you meet me at the dock? I'd like an escort down to the boat, and I don't know who else to call." I ran the words out like a record on high speed.

"Slow down there, Whit. What's going on?"

I thought about giving him a brief rundown as I made my way to his house three streets over, but I didn't have enough time before I arrived. I'd rethought the escort to the boat because now I wanted an escort to the dock itself first.

Who had left me this rock? The Franklins? The Aherns? Which family and what did they have to hide? Other than a murderer, I supposed.

"I'm almost at your house. Can you just take me down to the dock and then come on the cruise with me? I won't even charge you for the view of the glory of the bottom of the sea." I was babbling, and I knew it, and saying inane things, which I knew too. But I was scared.

I felt like I wanted to just blow it off and throw the rock

away, letting whoever had left it know they didn't worry me. I'd do whatever the heck I wanted, regardless of their scare tactics.

But I was also not going to be one of those heroines in a horror movie who was just too stupid to live when they ran into the attic with the fiend on their heels.

"I can come with you." He stepped out of his front door just as I pulled up at the curb.

I will totally cop to the fact that I ran into his arms and buried my head in his chest for just a minute. I'd barely even scratched the surface on this one and already the threats were coming in. At least last time they'd waited until I'd almost had the culprit before trying to hurt me.

"Now tell me what's going on," Felix said after a moment. He lifted my chin out of his shoulder and looked directly into my eyes.

"I . . . I . . ."

"Calm down first and then talk to me. What time do you have to be at the boat?"

That at least I could answer. "Less than thirty minutes."

"Okay, no time for a nice chat on the front porch. Why don't you get back in the golf cart and I'll drive you down to the dock. Then you can gather your thoughts to tell me what the heck is going on."

I took some deep breaths, nodded, and got into the cart. I really wasn't sure of what was scaring me so much about this. It was a rock. No one had thrown it through my window, or tried to use it to hurt me. They hadn't thrown it at me in the street to stone me to death.

And the words could have meant anything. Maybe there was someone else on the island who was selling the same kinds of rocks, and they thought I was infringing on their business in that way. It didn't have to be from one of the families.

Now I was just lying to myself to make me feel better, and that wouldn't do. But it also made me very aware that if whoever had dropped off the rock thought it would stop me from look-ing, they were way wrong. It only made me want to look harder. Someone knew Leo had not killed himself, and I was going to expose them for the evil jerk they were.

Felix held my hand the whole way to the harbor and rubbed his thumb over my fingers. It was a small gesture, and one I ap-preciated more than I could say.

He parked in the gravel near the pier and then turned side-ways to sit with one arm cocked on the steering wheel and the other across the back of the seat. He touched my shoulder and then left his hand there.

"Now spill. What on earth happened that has you so scared? And who do I have to take out snorkeling without a snorkel to make it go away?"

I laughed because I could and then leaned forward to hug him and kiss him on the cheek. "My knight in rubber-suited armor."

"I'll have you know I do have a harpoon too, if that matters. It might not be a lance or a sword, but it could work wonders."

"And make for yet one more murder to solve. I'm pretty sure I wouldn't want to have to find you after that."

"I'm sure we could blame it on someone else." He smiled but it got me to thinking. I'd hit upon a death in those archives that had been ruled an accident and it was one of the Franklins. Could the feud have something to do with that? Could the Aherns have been responsible for a death and managed to cover it up?

Because my head had been so full of everything all day, I had tucked a notebook into my bag and took it out now. I explained the situation to Felix as I wrote down my theory so I wouldn't forget.

"What should I do about this rock? I don't want to be stupid and not take it seriously, but it could mean anything. I don't want to stop looking for the killer just because someone thinks

I'm getting too close. My concern too, is what will this person do if I actually do get close?" I didn't want to sound like a coward, but these were valid concerns. As much as I wanted justice, I also wanted to make it through alive.

"I think you take care and do the things you know you can do while watching your back. I'll be watching it too, and so will Maribel."

I hugged him close and then held his hand as we walked down to the beach. I slipped my sneakers off and let my toes sink into the sand and just stood for a moment. This was what I had been missing living in Long Beach. Yeah, I could still get to the beach when I had lived there, but it could take forever to find a parking spot, then to stake out a piece of sand that wouldn't be overrun by kids and blankets and towels and coolers.

Here it was low-key and accessible, and I loved it. And that was going to have to be enough. The rest I'd leave up to the universe to sort out. I had my store, I had my boyfriend, and I had a mystery to solve once I got done with running the cruise. That was enough for now. The rest could wait until tomorrow. And if that rock-leaver thought they had scared me away with their black paint and vapid statement, then they were sorely mistaken.

"Okay, I can do this. I think some of my cruisers are making their way to the dock now. We should get down there to greet them and take vouchers. You're still going to take the cruise with me?" I felt better and ready to take on the cruising world at least.

"Of course. I always enjoy your spiel. We'll get them out into the ocean and grill anyone who looks suspicious."

After putting my shoes back on, I hooked my arm through his and we made our way over to the dock where about ten people were standing on either side of the wooden planks. They seemed to be facing off once I got closer and that made me pick up my pace because some of the faces looked familiar.

But it must have just been the light of the sinking sun. Once I got to the dock and put myself in the midst of the crowd, no one actually looked familiar. Ah, a cruise of all tourists. That was never a bad thing.

I escorted them all onto the *Sea Bounder* and then closed off the gate behind Felix, who took a seat at the very back.

It looked like it was several groups of two and three people. That also would work in my favor and would allow me to give my speech while giving myself some breathing time away from the mystery. At least for the next hour I could simply settle into the known and leave the unknown on shore.

"Everyone grab a seat and position yourselves so you'll be able to see through the glass wells in the floor." After I cautioned them against trying to get into the well itself, we took off. Backing the boat into the ocean, I started by pointing out the coral reefs and the fish swimming by.

I needed this time of peace and normalcy to gather my thoughts and get myself back to where I wanted to be. It never helped for me to get riled up when I should be thinking clearly.

There were some oohs and ahhs, and I briefly thought back to the time those turned into shrieks at the sight of a shark swimming under the boat.

This time would be placid and uneventful, even if I had to rope everyone down into their chairs.

"So what do you think about the feud?" Felix said over the radio to me. He'd chosen a frequency that didn't go throughout the cabin, and for that I was thankful, even though I had really just wanted to talk to the passengers and not have to think too much about what was going on back on land.

"I have no idea, and it appears no one else does either. How is it that no one can know and yet still be fighting over it? You know that's what happened in Romeo and Juliet too. No one ever said why the Montagues and Capulets were fighting."

"You wouldn't have let that stand if it had been you in there."

I muffled my laughter so as not to call attention to myself. "I have to get back to my tour. Save your thoughts for later. We can go get a cup of coffee or something." I picked up the microphone for the cabin. "If you look below us now you'll see a whole bunch of fish feeding on the reef. They like to go out in the evening and often will follow the lights we installed in the windows just to get a peek at us too."

The kids squealed and brought a sense of peace to me that I hadn't had since this whole thing started. I wanted justice for Leo, I wanted his killer found, and I wanted my island to go back to being a safe place. Being on the boat had given me the reprieve I needed, and now it was time to get down to business.

"We're heading back to the harbor. Wave goodbye to the fishes and that adorable octopus who just decided he wanted in on the action."

I pulled up to the dock a few minutes later and breathed a sigh of relief. No angst, no searching, no surprises. That was what I wanted again when this was all over, but it wouldn't be possible until I got some more information and more ideas about who could have killed that poor man.

I had work to do. Work that required I dig back in to the past and see why on earth the Aherns and the Franklins were still at war on such a small island almost one hundred years later.

I escorted everyone off the boat, then made sure the whole thing was empty and spiffed up before Felix and I left.

Walking up the dock, we held hands as I rested my head on his shoulder. "You wanted to know what I thought of this feud? Honestly, I think it's stupid, and I bet they wouldn't be fighting if they knew what started the whole thing in the first place. In the meantime, I have to keep looking."

"We're helping too. Maribel said that things are proceeding at the station as if it was a suicide, and Barney has every intention of shutting this whole thing down, so just be careful. I think Ray Pablano might have a thing or two to say about that, though. A rock on your front seat with a warning and fake dripping blood isn't exactly getting pushed into a gully, but it's not something to ignore either."

"I get it. I just wish I knew what it meant."

"I can tell you," a voice said out of the dark, and I held on tighter to Felix. A shadow separated from the side of my golf cart. Jake Ahern, the park ranger from yesterday and the brute of this morning, stood not five feet from me with another leer on his face. I was never so happy to have Felix with me.

"What do you want, Jake? I don't have time for more of your posturing. If you've got something to say, say it, and get lost. I didn't like your tone earlier today, and I probably won't like it now, either."

My words seemed to stop him in his tracks and the smirk dropped off his face. He took two steps closer in a powerful stride. I did everything I could not to hide behind Felix and just let him take the guy on himself. I was made of stronger stuff than that.

So I stepped out in front even as Felix tried to tug me back. I ended up toe to toe with Jake. His face appeared more tired than it had before, and he looked like he'd been beaten down—not physically but emotionally.

"Whit, I want to talk with you, and I can tell you what that rock is for, but I need you to listen with an open mind, and maybe give me at least a little credit for being a decent human being, or you're never going to believe what I have to tell you."

I struggled with that for a moment, but he really did look like he'd been put through the wringer. "I'll try, but so far you haven't done much to make me believe that you're not just going along with the party line. Why on earth did you call your family in despite saying you were going to call the cops? Which you didn't, for the record. I did."

"It's all a big misunderstanding, I promise. I'm trying to do what's right, but you have no idea how hard that is to do."

"I've been in that position a time or two myself, Jake," Felix chimed in. "We'll give you the floor and try to listen with open ears, but I really hope you have something more to say than you were coerced or pressured."

"What about joining us for coffee?" It was the best I could come up with as the moon rode high in the sky and places started closing down for the night.

Once the last ferry left from the harbor, things got quieter and quieter on the island. We had some nightlife in restaurants and at private homes, but not a ton of shops stayed open late. At that time, in the middle of the week, we might only get one or two customers, if we were lucky, and if they weren't too drunk to do anything more than crash around in the store.

"Could we do ice cream instead?" Jake asked. "I'm feeling a craving for something stronger, but I've got to keep my head on straight if I'm going to tell you everything I know and get myself out of the running on what I expect is your very long suspect list."

Chapter 13

Settled in on a bench out at the beach, Felix and I bookended Jake between us. I took my first luscious bite of chocolate peanut butter ice cream in a homemade waffle cone. I'd asked for sprinkles too, and Garry Templeton, owner of the Daily Scoop, was extremely generous with the shaker.

I let us all sit for just a few moments and enjoy the soft breeze as night settled over the island and the streetlights came on. The moon reflected in all her glory over the ocean and the wavelets at the shore kept up a rhythm that would have normally put me to sleep.

I leaned my head back for just a second, then took another bite of my creamy snack.

Then it was time to get some answers.

"All right, the little interlude is done. We've got ice cream, I'm feeling as mellow and open as I possibly can be, so talk, Jake. What's going on and what do you have to get off your chest?"

"To the point." He used a napkin to wipe the side of his mouth.

Felix used another napkin to get the corner of his own mouth, then reached past Jake to hand me another once since I'd forgotten mine. "To be fair, she gave you at least a few minutes without breaking into the questions."

"That is true." Jake took another bite of his ice cream and I waited, quite patiently I might add, for him to start with the words. "Give me a second."

He took another bite of ice cream out of his bowl and stared out over the ocean. The sparkle of the stars in the sky and the puffy clouds scudding through the dark made for a beautiful picture, but I could be enjoying this from my deck instead of down here waiting for the guy who'd sought me out to start with the talking.

"The family wanted to be called in, yes, but I'm not the one who actually did it. I just want to start there. I had my cell out to call the sheriff's office when my cousin showed up and took it from me. He's the one who sent out a group text to get everyone to the crime scene before the police were called."

He kept his eyes forward and his hands in his lap. Without eye contact I couldn't tell if he was trying to pull one over on me, but that could wait until he had the whole story out.

"So you admit it was a crime scene." I pounced on that one like it was the last peanut butter egg at Easter and the supply boat wasn't coming back for another two days.

"Yes, I do, even if the others don't want it to be. Currently, they're doing everything in their power to keep it ruled as nothing more than a suicide. But I guarantee you I'm not alone, and I can tell you that outside the rift with the Franklins, we're starting to have our own infighting over who did this and how it should be handled."

As he shook his head, I shot Felix a look. Infighting could definitely work in our favor because people wanted to tell their side when it came to that kind of thing. But I didn't need another explosion, and at least one of their clan was willing to kill if this wasn't a suicide and others were willing to keep it silent.

"Do you know what the feud is about?" It seemed to be the only question I really wanted answered other than who the killer was. And yet I wasn't even certain that it would help if I knew.

It could have been some social slight, like not being invited to a dinner party, or maybe that one election I'd read about at the newspaper where the Franklins had won the vote for mayor about fifty years ago. They'd promptly changed everything to their favor. But then the Aherns had won two years later and changed everything back to the way they wanted, the one that benefited them the most.

Then again, it could have absolutely nothing to do with the current situation.

I had to remember that and not get so laser-focused on the feud that I forgot there could be other reasons and other suspects.

But man, did I want to know what the feud had been about and hoped that it was enough to still be running even to this day.

"I wish I *did* know," Jake said. "I think it involves a lie somehow. That's what my mom had said once. But she was also drunk and not quite in her right mind. It stuck with me all these years, though, so it might have some truth to it. She'd never talk again after that one time."

A drunken lady's words were not something I could pin a case on.

"So you did ask again but she never said anything else? Did you try asking her recently?"

He shrugged. "It probably wouldn't do any good. She doesn't remember much anymore, and I'm doing everything I can to keep her at home with her Alzheimer's. If I can't care for her, then I'm going to have to send her to the mainland for continued care."

I hadn't realized it had gotten that far with his mother. I didn't remember them much since they hadn't lived here when I was a teenager, but they came over after his mother had won the lottery or won big at a casino on the mainland or something based on Goldy's island gossip. That wasn't important, though. What was important was seeing if we could jog her memory about the old days without hurting her.

I felt a little off about asking, but it might need to be done if only to get me away from the family feud and onto a new suspect once I had an answer.

"Can we talk to her? I promise to be gentle and not agitate her, but if she knows something then she might be the only one."

He shrugged again. "She'd like visitors."

We talked times for the next day and then he didn't have much more to say. He got up to leave when I remembered that we'd started talking because he'd said he knew who had put that rock on my front seat on the golf cart.

"Wait, the rock-leaver?" I said as he walked away.

He turned back around and waved. "Maybe think a little outside the box."

"The person who left the rock!" I yelled. "You said you knew who it was!"

He shrugged—it seemed to be his signature move—and wandered off down the road. I didn't have the energy to go after him. Felix did, though, but I shook my head no when he looked to me.

"What the heck does that mean?" I asked Felix. "Do you think he knows and doesn't want to tell us, or did he just use it as a way to tell his side of the story in the hopes I would think he was a good guy just being taken advantage of?"

Felix shrugged. "Maybe he just wanted free ice cream." I smacked him in the arm. He laughed then said, "It could be both. Maybe he doesn't know anything about the rock. We were talking about it as we made our way to your golf cart, so it's possible he just overheard and used it as an intro. Then again, he might know exactly who left it, and getting you to believe he isn't a bad guy could throw off suspicion. I'm thinking we might want to look into his history a little more."

"Ugh, another name to research. I guess I'll add it to the list."

"You know, you could spread some of it around. I've been offering to help and so has Maribel, but I'm not really seeing much from you in the way of asking other than when you practically flew to my house with a random rock."

He had a point. I needed to let go of the reins a little if I wanted to get this solved before the suicide was ruled and the case was closed. Although, I had looked into what steps were needed if a suicide was later proved to be murder. It could be reopened. It just would take a hell of a lot of fancy footwork and legalese to make it happen.

"You're absolutely right, and don't you dare complain about how much work I'm expecting out of you when I email you tonight." I nudged him with my shoulder. "I think I'm going to pass on the coffee since I just had the ice cream. I'll go home to make that list now and we'll get cracking. We have little time and a ton to do. I hope you're up to this."

"Babe, I've got your back." He wrapped his arms around me and rested his chin on my head. "I signed on for all of it. Even with the murders that seem to keep cropping up, this is the best life I've lived in a long time. It's no secret that you're one of the primary reasons I feel that way. If this is important to you, then it's important to me too. Not to mention I'd love to get one over on Barney Warrington and help Ray."

"To one over on Barney, then."

I dropped him back off at his house and then zoomed my

way back to my own home. I'd make that list and then separate it out, hopefully in a way that didn't have us all doing double-duty research on top of one another. There had to be something that led to the killer. And we were going to find it. High water, here I came.

I marched into my house like I was going to battle to find Maribel asleep on the couch with Whiskers curled up on top of her head. Well, that was one down for the count.

I quietly made my way back to my bedroom and closed the door. I didn't want to disturb her and tomorrow was soon enough to see if she had new information. Right now I had lists to make.

I grabbed my research from the newspaper office and focused in again on the lack of money but breadth of spending in the twenties. For some reason that just kept jumping out at me.

I put it aside for a moment, winged out a list of people for Felix to look into—which he promptly replied with a bon voyage—and then I settled in with my own list.

What had been going on in the twenties here? I pulled up website after website about Catalina. For such a small island we did have quite a bit of research done on us over the years. There were books that I carried in the store, but those were more about the landscape and the wildlife around here. What about the social aspect?

And then I hit on a few that mentioned Prohibition. I'd been more of a Shakespeare time period person and the 1920s and '30s had not been my thing at all. I knew peripherally what the highlights of the early twentieth century were, but not the nitty gritty.

I was about to get into the nitty gritty, though, when I saw a familiar last name on page two of an article and the words MOONSHINE IN CATALINA.

Could this be the big feud? Could it have to do with illegal activities and the fact that the Aherns had been cops for years and the Franklins were making illegal alcohol under their noses and making money off of it hand over fist?

Could that be the lie Jake had referenced?

I settled in after making myself some popcorn as quietly as possible, even pulling it from the microwave three seconds early so as not to wake up my best friend. I hoped she appreciated that in the morning when she finally woke up.

I scrolled and used keywords to find more information. It did look like the Franklins had been involved in illegal alcohol making. They'd been known to also use their private boats to sail it across the channel to get it to Los Angeles. Some pretty well-known people had admitted to it being the best they'd ever tasted.

Well, after Prohibition was over in 1933, of course.

I found one small mention of an arrest and a fight but little else. And then I considered shutting down for the night because I was getting nowhere and this was not helping me. It might have something to do with the family feud, but information from almost a hundred years ago was not going to help me find a killer today unless it was a ghost.

Back to the basics, then. I had Manny to talk to, Aaron to corner, and Leo's girlfriend, Janina, to question, along with any other amount of people that I hadn't thought of because I'd been so wrapped up in the feud that I hadn't really looked for individuals.

That wasn't to say that someone from the other family hadn't done the killing, but it had to be something more than just the feud. They had to have chosen Leo for a reason other than something that did or did not happen one hundred years ago.

I moved out to the couch where Maribel had been sleeping and knuckled down at almost midnight. She must have gotten up and gone to her room at some point. Settling into the comfy cushions, I made my list of lists. I had tomorrow to get all my ducks in a row and start searching out some info to find a killer or this would go down as a suicide.

From what I remembered of Leo, golfing was the last thing I'd have expected him to be doing. He'd been into football in high school and could fish in his sleep, but golf had not been something he'd ever done. So why a golf course?

Chapter 14

I woke up to the sound of Maribel banging around in the kitchen and found myself facedown on the couch across from where she had been sleeping only hours ago.

"I'm making scrambled eggs, if you want any!" she yelled from the kitchen. There was absolutely no need to yell with how small our house was, but she did it anyway.

"Murph," I mumbled as I stuck my head back into the pillows on the back of the couch. My neck hurt and my hip wasn't doing so well either, from being buried in the couch cushions. I hadn't even had the forethought to make myself marginally comfortable before drifting off in the middle of my notes.

Speaking of notes . . . I grabbed my notebook from under my elbow and found the pages were creased and half the words were illegible. I must have been fighting sleep and writing at the same time. Awesome.

"You sure you don't want any while we talk about the things I found out last night?" Maribel said from the kitchen in a normal tone this time. At least she wasn't yelling anymore. "Sorry about not being awake for the eight o'clock thing. So much happened, and I just couldn't keep my eyes open. Thanks for not waking me."

She emerged from the kitchen with a skillet in one hand. Those eggs did smell delicious and might be just the thing I needed to get my poor brain working in the right direction.

I had at least had the foresight, at about two in the morning, to text Goldy and ask her to run the store today. I checked my phone and found her response in the affirmative before dragging myself off the couch and into one of the chairs at our dining room table.

"Ketchup?" Maribel asked.

"You know me so well."

"I don't want to be interrupted before we even get into all the good bits, so it's better to have all the necessities out of the way first and then jump in."

She must not have slept with her face buried in pillows and her rear end stuck between cushions. She was bright-eyed and bushy-tailed, and I tried not to hate her for it. Instead, I put ketchup on my eggs, gladly took the plate of bacon from her, and pulled a chocolate chip muffin from the basket she'd put on the table before I woke up.

"What's all this for?" I asked, splitting open my muffin to see which half had more chocolate chips. That's the one I'd eat last. "We don't normally do breakfast this big. I'm a smoothie kind of girl or one of those energy bars, and so are you."

She seated herself before covering her lap in a napkin. She'd taken the time to get dressed and I was still wearing what I had on last night. Thank goodness this was a no-judgment zone.

Pulling the basket toward her, she picked out a muffin that looked like it had more chips than mine. "I thought a change of pace might be a good thing for both of us right now. We have a case to solve, and let me tell you that if I can get one over on that Barney I will be one happy camper. He's blocking my request for additional training because he doesn't like that I'm friends with you, so I am going to show him a thing or two." She ripped open that poor muffin with far more force than necessary.

"I'll gladly take your vindictiveness as long as it's directed toward someone else and helps me get out of this rut I've stuck myself into. I can't seem to get away from the feud. It's like an obsession at this point, and I really need to stop focusing on it today and get down to the people who could have actually killed Leo."

"I'd heard that you were asking a bunch of questions about that. And that you went to the newspaper office. Good thought, but not what we need at the moment."

"You're telling me."

"I am telling you." She smiled as she served herself eggs and then peeled the paper off another muffin. "I'm also telling you that we're looking in the wrong direction. We might not know what started the family feud, but I will tell you it is alive and well. Those two star-crossed lovers were getting harassed continuously and threatened if they didn't stay away from each other."

"Really? I hadn't heard. I think Goldy would have said something if she knew."

"But she didn't even know they were dating from what you told me." Leaning forward, she picked up her coffee cup. "The information I'm getting is that this was all kept very under wraps to anyone on the outside. I don't know how your grandfather got wind of it in the first place."

"He said someone told him in passing. Go on. Who's doing the harassing?"

"Both sides from what I understand. My dinner with Fabian might have been exhausting last night, but it wasn't a total waste of time. I even made him pay before he took a phone call."

She smirked and I put my hand up for a high five. "Nicely done."

"Ha! Thanks. I won't be doing that again, though, so don't ask."

"Once was definitely enough."

"Good. Getting back to the rest of the information he gave me. Her family for betraying them and his family for thinking he can do better. But now he's gone."

"Has anyone talked to his mom?" I figured it was worth asking since Maribel would know better than any member of my other cobbled-together team.

"Poor Judith. She's a mess. Every time I see her she looks like she wants to crawl inside a hole and leave the world behind. But she clings to Aaron instead. They're rarely apart."

"That's Aaron's sister-in-law, right?"

"Yes, and he seems to be her only support at the moment. Everyone on the Franklin side wants the killer found, but there have been rumblings that this would have never happened if Leo had just stuck with more acceptable women."

My heart ached for him. No one should be told who they can love. "I'll see if I can find any more, but that sounds like it goes to motive for the Aherns even more. What else have you got?" I picked up my own cup and delighted in the smell of Earl Grey tea. Maribel was an amazing roommate.

"Next, despite all the time he's been spending with Judith, it seems Aaron apparently has a girlfriend he doesn't want anyone to know about. She was who he was supposed to be meeting when he was supposedly bird-watching. He could be covering up for a significant other. Maybe she's also from the Ahern clan. He's never dated anyone as far as I was told, but this could be an issue. So we need to look there and I might have a lead on finding out who she was."

"Do tell."

She crumbled more of her muffin onto the plate. "I can tell you, but I'm not really going to be able to help you with the finding out because it could be considered illegal."

"So I can do illegal things but not you? How's that work out for me in the end?" And why did everyone seem to think that putting me in dangerous spots was okay as long as their hands got to stay clean?

"You have more leeway." She stuck her elbows on the glass-topped table we'd saved from a garage sale when we got here. "I want to get Barney and help Ray, but I also want to keep my job. And all those crime shows we watch might have people who don't lose their jobs when they step out of line, but that's not how the real world works. I don't want to have to go back to living with my mom."

I snorted and almost bobbled my tea. "I'd never let you leave the island, even if you didn't have a job. We'd figure something out."

Patting my hand, she smiled. "And I appreciate that more than I can say, but I want to be responsible for myself. I just need to be a little irresponsible with some information I came across."

"Okay." I dug into the eggs and then closed my eyes and hummed in appreciation. "Did you put cheese in these?"

"You know I did. I wouldn't have offered them to you with anything less."

"Well, I appreciate it." I took another bite, then opened my notebook. "So what do you have that I'm going to have to look into since you can't?"

"Actually, it might have come from your Pops when I saw him and Goldy at dinner last night."

"So she did talk him into taking her out for an engagement anniversary. I never doubted it." I chuckled because that was classic Goldy.

"Yes. I stopped by their table once the bill was paid and he was very chatty. He said that Aaron had asked him to put out a box for someone to find about two weeks ago and it contained a ring."

My mind raced as I tried to remember selling that to him. And I did remember after a few more bites of the delicious eggs and a strip or two of bacon. He'd come into the Dame of the Sea asking if he could take one of the boxes he'd already made me and I agreed. "Okay, so we have a box but I would have no idea how to find out who it was hidden for. And I wouldn't even know where to start looking for that information, especially if it's already been buried and dug up."

"But it was supposed to be buried today."

"And you think that if I go put it out the person will pick it up? Aaron might not have told her ahead of time that they should lay low."

"Pops said that he was supposed to be the one who delivered the chest to a special place today and then call the woman and let her know it was there."

I chewed on that for a moment as I popped several chunks of muffin into my mouth. Wouldn't that be cruel, though, to bury the chest when I fully intended to spy on the person picking it up and use the information to nail a murderer? I felt like that would be crass. And told Maribel as much.

"I just don't know," I said. "Maybe we could bury a chest and put something in it for Janina and have it come from Leo to get her away from her family." Leo's girlfriend was one of the top people on my list that I needed to speak with if I could figure out how to get her alone.

"And you don't think that would be crass?" Maribel frowned. "That's worse than outing a hidden relationship. It's one thing to get a message from the grave unintentionally, like an envelope that never got sent to the right house finally showing up years later, but Leo is still on a slab down at the station. I don't think I could do that to Janina."

"And that's exactly what I would have told Pops if he ever called me. But he talked to you instead, so we're going to have to come up with something else." I stuck my elbows on the table. "So the thought is to call this woman, or find out who she is by using her number, and then asking her about what she knows.

That might be more helpful than hurtful. Though I'm not entirely sure why they are hiding things."

"Unless they're from the two families and might have helped Leo along . . ."

"Right."

"And then we'd have the killer anyway, and she wouldn't deserve any of our sympathy." Maribel wiped the corners of her mouth with her napkin, then placed it on the table.

"Do you have the number?" I grabbed my cell phone and pulled up the software I'd purchased for the store. It helped when I got phone calls I missed or if I wanted to track a supplier and find out where they were located if the information wasn't readily available on the internet.

"Of course I do. What is it with you thinking I'm not always prepared? I might not have been a Girl Scout, but I've got the skills down without the badges."

She handed over the number, and I stared at it for a moment to see if I might recognize it. But let's be honest, I hadn't memorized a number in years and knew that if I ever lost my phone I would be very much out of luck because I knew no one's number by heart anymore. I barely remembered my own sometimes.

Using the search engine, I typed in the number and came up with a man's name, Raul Jorge Martinez, and an address I hadn't been to in years: Middle Ranch Road, which runs through the center of the island. Not that I was against a man proposing to a man but everyone had kept saying "girlfriend" and "proposing to a woman" that I was taken off guard for a moment.

I put the number in again to verify and came up with the same info. Along with a work address that I was more familiar with: La Annaffiare, the restaurant where Sylvie worked. The one she owned.

So was Aaron secretly dating someone in her employ, or was it Sylvie and she was hiding because of that darn family feud?

There was only one way to find out and that was to go on

down to the restaurant and ask. I wasn't taking a chance on her not answering the phone or texting her and having her ignore it.

"Even though a man's name is on the actual phone number, I think it's Sylvie. Maybe she had a fake phone so that her family wouldn't find out that she was dating a Franklin. That's got to be it. I can feel it in my gut."

"You have got to stop watching *NCIS*, Gibbs, and get into the real world. You can't just go stomping in there and demand answers from someone who obviously thought things needed to be hidden. Not to mention you still have other people to look into. Maybe someone else found out about Sylvie dating a Franklin and killed Leo to warn everyone what can happen if they don't put a stop to this thing."

"That's stretching it," I said. Whiskers, in all her fluffy glory, decided we had been ignoring her too long and came up under my hand to demand pets.

Frowning at me, Maribel crossed her arms over her chest. "It could happen."

I put my head down on the table and breathed in. Yeah, running in like the building was on fire would be a bad idea and would probably scare her off. Measured and calculated was a much better approach.

But how?

Maribel and I spent some more time going over the logistics and once I felt confident in what I was going to say and how I'd present myself, I went to get dressed.

The drive to the closed restaurant would have taken a few seconds but I didn't want anyone to know I was there by seeing my distinctive golf cart parked out front, and I thought I'd use the extra time walking to work my way through my thoughts now that I had a plan. I dropped the rock off in my desk as I went past the store, just to get it out of my hands.

If Aaron's girlfriend was in fact Sylvie then I thought they would make an adorable couple. Perhaps it would also bring closure to things that had been going on way too long, like Leo and Janina would have if given the chance.

But if it was someone else, I didn't want to come off looking like an idiot. Hence the walk to the restaurant to give myself time to work my way through every single scenario I could think of.

But when I got there and went around back, it was to find a bedraggled and crying Sylvie hyperventilating like she was inhaling from a scuba tank that wasn't giving out enough PSIs.

I stepped back before she saw me and rethought my plan. I got jabbed in the back for my trouble, and then hid behind the bush that had assaulted me. The scent of gardenias rose from the petals in wafts.

How could I possibly go in and make this worse for her? I didn't know her well enough to say I was stopping in to check on her. And I hadn't been around often in that casual drop-by manner to just duck in and ask what was wrong. Heck, I couldn't even afford to eat at her restaurant more than every once in a while for a special occasion, so it wasn't like we even had that in common.

I gnawed on my lip until it felt raw. And in the process heard a door open and close. Had I missed my opportunity to talk with her? Had she gone inside?

At least I could have just happened past her by accident when she was sitting outside if I'd stayed my course. Now I couldn't exactly knock on the front door and hope she answered, and then stumble my way through an explanation that I'd seen her but hadn't had the heart to ask what was wrong.

Damn!

"Babe, you have to stop doing this to yourself." A male voice said the words in a lowered voice. I wasn't sure who it was and couldn't exactly sneak a look. But I wasn't going anywhere if Sylvie was still outside sobbing and no one else was around.

"I can't. How the hell am I going to recover from this? I had so many plans. So many things I wanted to do. So many things we were going to do together and now it's all over. Why is it always like this, Georgie?"

Ah, okay, George Martin, her head bartender.

"I don't know, but killing yourself out here isn't going to make it better."

"At least I don't have to take all the calls I know are going to be coming in the future, and I won't have to think about him every time I turn around and see that freaking vase on the end of the bar."

"We could just put the vase away. He won't be coming in to see it anymore anyway, so it's not like he'll say anything about it not being there. Why torture yourself?"

"Why did I torture myself from the beginning? I should never have taken his call after all those years. Things wouldn't be so messed up right now if I had just let that go to voice mail. He built so many things up in my head and now he's gone and took it all with him."

There was more sobbing and a big cloud of cigarette smoke blew out my way around the corner. I put my hand over my mouth and nose because the last thing I wanted to do was cough or sneeze when I was this close.

Part of me felt bad for spying on them and eavesdropping on a conversation that was obviously not meant for my ears. However, if I got some answers or some direction then it couldn't all be bad.

"I just don't know what I'm going to do now," Sylvie said, but it sounded muffled. Maybe George was hugging her or maybe she'd lowered her head to her crossed arms. I so wished I had one of those around-the-corner mirrors, or even a convenient little drone camera, but that would be taking my so-called hobby just a little too far.

"You soldier on like you've done before. And at least now he won't be putting his hands all over you."

My ears perked up. Why wouldn't she want her boyfriend's hands on her if he was about to give her a ring and, I assumed, ask her to marry him? Wasn't that the whole point of marriage? Intimacy, someone you loved who would hold you and love you?

Things had just gotten a lot more interesting.

I leaned around the corner, making sure I still couldn't be seen, yet giving myself the best vantage point possible to hear the conversation from the gardenia bush.

"He wasn't that bad. And I only needed him until things got off the ground. The money he's been sending to me has helped in so many ways. If he wanted a kiss now and then, it wasn't the end of the world. Fortunately, he was old-fashioned and was fine with waiting until after the wedding for more. I would have figured that part out when it was time."

"Did you at least get the last installment?" George asked.

"I thought there was one today, but with Leo dead I highly doubt that's going to happen now."

"Ah, yes, Leo. At least that's one thing taken care of." I couldn't tell from his voice if that was a derisive comment or one of relief. I wished I could see their faces, but I couldn't risk it.

I made mental notes because at this point I was barely breathing so I wouldn't miss a word. I certainly didn't want to miss something while I was scribbling away.

So an installment she was waiting for that wouldn't happen with Leo gone, a man she didn't love even though he had loved her, and some future plans that were now thwarted due to an untimely death and not wanting to actually be with the boyfriend in the first place.

Had she wanted to just keep stringing Aaron along but something about Leo's death now made that impossible? Or was she aware of the upcoming ring? Had she had someone kill Leo and make it look like suicide to get out of marrying Aaron since she knew for a fact she wasn't willing to go that far?

But how did it all tie in together?

My brain was getting crammed again with information and that was the only thing I could point to as to why I didn't hear my grandmother calling my name until she was almost on top of me. And with the name-calling, chairs scraped around the corner, a cigarette butt flew out my way, and the back door slammed shut.

Chapter 15

"Well, shoot." It wasn't quite what I wanted to say, but since I never swore in front of Goldy I wasn't going to start now.

"Why didn't you answer me, Whit? I must have called your name three times, and you didn't even turn around." She huffed up alongside me with her indignation flying like a red flag. All I could do was cover my eyes with my palm so she couldn't see them rolling like a pair of dice on a craps table.

"Whitney Dagner, I am talking to you. The least you could do is acknowledge me. And if you have earbuds in again, you and I are going to have the talk about the dangers of not being aware of your surroundings."

I finally turned around and gave her a grimace. "Let's move this away from here," I said quietly. Maybe there was still something to be salvaged. Goldy hadn't called out where I was standing. Maybe George and Sylvie could have just gone in because someone was out somewhere on the street. Goldy could have been calling to me from a block away going the opposite direction.

I wasn't sure I totally believed that myself, but it could work with the right spin, and if I could keep myself from stumbling over a lie like I usually did.

I grabbed her arm to move her along the sidewalk and away from any windows on the restaurant. My story wouldn't hold up if I walked by, and although I was sure Sylvie hadn't seen me, I couldn't chance it.

"I'm not taking another step until you tell me what on earth you are doing, young lady." Goldy dug in her heels—and I do mean heels, all four inches of them—into the wooden boardwalk and refused to budge. So I let go of her arm and just kept on walking and waited for her to catch up.

Sure enough, I heard the tattoo of her picking up speed to get to me as we crossed over to the grocery store parking lot. I took her another block along the road, then sat down on the bench Phil Mayhew had outside his house.

It was a mermaid and a merman with their tails intertwined and holding hands. It was a beautiful piece, and one tourists did not sit on normally. But since I did indeed know Phil, I also knew he was out of town for the week. I felt that it was as safe a place as any to talk.

Checking my temper and my irritation at the bench, I took a deep breath before I began. "I didn't answer because I was listening to Sylvie talk about how she wasn't sure how she was going to make ends meet. And how she isn't getting another installment payment—not unless, I think, it's in the treasure box her boyfriend is going to have delivered tonight. But I'm pretty sure that box has a ring in it. Not to mention that he supposedly took off and left her with nothing. The boyfriend in question being Aaron Franklin." Those weren't exactly the words she had used, but I had a gut feeling I was right nonetheless.

"Wait, Sylvie? Sylvie was the one Aaron was going to propose to? How did I miss that? I was here to tell you that Janina works at the golf course. That's her supposed moonlighting."

"Really? Maybe I can catch her there, then. And to answer your question, I don't think anyone knew. Sylvie was talking to George the bartender, but that could have just been because he was available and the whole thing was over now. I don't know."

I plucked at the tines of the merman's crown. "It sounded like she had these plans all set up and thought she'd get money today. But with Leo's death something changed." Again not exactly the words, but I was extrapolating and trying to make sense of it in my head.

"So she doesn't really love him? That's sad. He was going all out for her from what Thomas said. Being that he's my husband he should have told me long before now, but since he talked with Maribel he thought that maybe it was okay to reveal the secret he's been holding for weeks." She harrumphed and I sighed.

So Pops had thought to spill to Maribel and talk with Goldy but hadn't said a word to me. I guessed that was to be expected, since he would have assumed that either one of them would have said something to me at some point.

Still, it would have been nice to talk to him myself because I had questions. A lot of them.

"Where is Pops now?"

"Burying some new chest for a tourist I sold it to this morning. And don't worry about the shop. I closed for a lunch hour to come see how you were doing."

"You couldn't just have called?"

"I tried three times and you didn't pick up, so I thought I'd come find you myself. It worked too."

"Yeah, and got me almost caught by my best lead yet."

"You can get the lead back. In fact, I bet we could walk into the restaurant right now, find Sylvie with her makeup a mess, and ask her how she's doing. Then you can simply lead off with that."

She was up before I could stop her. And despite the fact that

I had sneakers on and she was in four-inch heels, she still beat me to the front door of the restaurant.

Banging on the door, she also called out Sylvie's name as if the owner of the restaurant couldn't hear the banging. Behind her back, I rolled my eyes at Goldy, since it was the only safe place to roll them from.

I was pretty sure the banging on the door and expecting a wrecked Sylvie to come running wasn't going to work that way.

It didn't. Sylvie wasn't the one who ultimately answered the door when the people inside must have realized Goldy had no intention of stopping until someone acknowledged that she was there and insisting on being let in.

"Hi, Mrs. Dagner, what can I do for you?"

I had to give George points for the smile and the way he did not come storming out of the restaurant demanding why she was being such a nuisance. He'd answered with professionalism and an air of this was the first time he'd heard her at the door. I might have to work on that ability to deal with my own customers.

"Oh, George, good, I was hoping you might be here. I really messed up, my grandson and I desperately need to have an event catered. Could you maybe let us in so we can talk about what it would take to have a floating bar and appetizers aboard the *Bounder* for tonight? It should only take a few minutes, if you have a moment or two?"

That lilt at the end making it a soft question was ingenious. He smiled at her and took the towel on his shoulder and thwapped it back over his shoulder.

"For you I always have time, Goldy. I see you found Whitney."

And there was the jab that let us know he was on to us. Unless Goldy was quick enough to not let him know what we knew.

"Yes, my word, I didn't realize how loud I was if you could hear me all the way over here. She was coming out of the grocery store and I wanted to catch her before she went back to the shop. This one can be hard to get a hold of lately."

That smile was transferred to me. "I don't doubt it." He thwapped the towel again. I couldn't tell if he was going along with our story to see what we wanted, or if he truly believed Goldy. I'd have believed her. And I should have never doubted that she'd be able to lie with the best of them.

"If you need us to come back later we can do that." I tucked my hands into my shorts pockets. "We just thought it might be easier to talk when the restaurant wasn't open since it's so last minute."

See, that wasn't a lie and so it tripped right off my tongue. The smile this time no longer had an edge to it. Maybe we'd pulled it off. But this was going to cost a fortune, plus we had to find people to actually invite to the cruise with alcohol and appetizers.

He let us into the bar and gave us sodas. We sat down and every once in a while I glanced over George's shoulder to see if I could catch a glimpse of Sylvie to ask how she was doing. But she never showed and fifteen minutes later we had the whole thing set up, our drinks were drained, and we no longer had a reason to hang around.

"Thank you so much for helping out with this, George. I can't tell you how much you have saved my hide. Nick would have had a fit if he'd realized I completely forgot to set up the food and drinks. You're a lifesaver."

"It's not the first time, Goldy. We're happy to help. We'll see you tonight then at the dock."

"Yes, we'll be there. Have a good day and thanks again for taking this on. I know it's not exactly easy to do double duty.

Please tell Sylvie and the staff how much we appreciate you fitting us in. There'll be a generous tip for all of you."

And wouldn't that just make my grandfather happy, or Nick, depending on who was going to actually pay for this fake cruise with its real food and no actual guests.

I followed along behind Goldy as she exited the restaurant and shook my head once we were halfway down the street. "That did not help us at all, and now we're going to owe a ton of money for something that doesn't exist."

"Oh, darling, don't even worry about that. They'll get it done, and Sylvie is going to have to come out to deliver it because they have a big party tonight that George is bartending. Sylvie won't trust anyone else with that much food—or that much money, for that matter—if I deliver on the tip for everyone. You'll get your chance at her. Now we just need to figure out who to invite and how to get them to come as if they had been invited days and days ago."

We split at the library so she could finish out her immense scheme, and I could decide what my next move was. I had no ideas a full twenty minutes later, so I called Felix to find out if he'd had any luck with anyone on his list.

"Whit, how's it going?" His voice was very bright, like he was with someone else and couldn't talk at the moment.

"Good, you?"

"Doing great. Out on the golf course with Harold Ahern and just getting in a few swings before we go for a scuba lesson. I thought I'd let him show me his favorite pastime before I put him through the paces. Our caddy's one of the best, though, so that's good. You know how it is."

"I do not and you sound fake. Is Janina there?"

He laughed at that and then he hung up on me. Okay, so he was making progress. I then called Maribel.

"How's it going out there?" In contrast to Felix's bright loud voice, Maribel sounded like she was whispering in a closet.

"Are you okay?" I asked.

"Yes, just hiding out for the moment. Barney is rampaging through the station looking for me, but I can't let him find me just yet. I have to have a cover story for why I was looking into Leo's bank account when I should have been answering the phones."

"Well, that's not good. Did you come up with anything yet?"

"No, and I'm about to get desperate. I'm in the girls' bathroom right now. But I can't stay here forever, you know."

And it hit me. "Tell him that there was a question from the insurance company due to not being able to pay out on the claim because of the suicide and they just wanted to ensure the cause of death."

"Oh, that's a great idea. And I was doing it today because it turns out the medical examiner will be here tomorrow and the insurance company needs to know today so they can begin working on the claim. Brilliant!" She yelled that last word, and I heard a door clank open behind her and then the toilet flush as she cursed and hung up on me.

Okay, then. I tapped my phone against my chin, trying to run through the phone call again. I hated to use the word *assume* again but I couldn't come up with a new one that meant the same thing.

So I was going to assume that when Maribel yelled she had caught the attention of Barney, and he had come in to find her in the bathroom where she cursed and then flushed the toilet to make it seem like she had had a valid reason to be in there.

I hope she read him the riot act for coming into the ladies' room when it was obviously occupied.

I also hoped she remembered the story we'd come up with and was able to make it convincing.

The confirmation that the medical examiner wouldn't be here for another day did make me feel only slightly better and gave me at least another twenty-four hours to find out what the heck had happened to Leo and how to prove it wasn't suicide.

I would do that best by being able to hand the police department a killer they couldn't deny.

I texted Nick just to make sure I'd checked in with my whole team, then walked down the street.

Now to go find a killer. I'd start with Sylvie. If I had to be straight with her about why I was asking, then so be it. Beating around the bush was not helping me get any further along, and there were things to be done and a timeline in which to do them. I didn't have the luxury of waiting until tonight. Plus, she'd be making all that food for Goldy, so a possible captive audience. I could work with that.

First stop, the restaurant. When I found Sylvie out back again I didn't hesitate to round the corner.

I did, however, hesitate to grill her like shrimp on the barby when I found her crying again.

"Hey, Sylvie. Are you okay?"

She wiped her eyes hastily and gave me a sharp look before she seemed to melt back into the patio chair next to the back door.

"You know what, Whit, I'm not, and I'm tired of trying to seem like I am. If it's not you it's going to be someone else who asks, so it might as well be you. I hear you're looking into Leo's death."

I expected to see another cigarette, but instead only got a light whiff of a flowery scent I hadn't smelled in years: Elizabeth Arden's Red Door perfume. It took me back to memories of my mom, who had been trying to find her signature scent. I never did know if she found it, since that was the last time I'd seen her and it was over twenty years ago.

I shook my head to clear it, and Sylvie laughed derisively. "Please don't try to lie to me. I saw you and your grandmother come in this morning. I know all about the order. Are you here to cancel it? I'm sure it was a lie, and quite honestly, I have no idea why George said we could do it when I couldn't even have all that food ready until at least tomorrow. I might be fast but I'm not that fast."

I shrugged. "So do it for tomorrow. That'll give Goldy time to actually put together a party that deserves the food I'm sure you're going to make, and it would be a shame for it to go to waste."

Staring at me, she shook her head. "Well, when you go for honesty you go all the way, don't you? I guess you were standing right outside the patio instead of at the grocery store?"

"No, I wasn't." I kept my eyes on her and my tone sincere. I hadn't been right outside the patio since I was technically stashed in the gardenia bush.

Laughing, she turned more fully toward me. "You were doing so well there. Don't start lying now."

I shrugged. "I was actually around the corner in the gardenia bush."

That got her to laugh more fully and seem to settle back into her chair.

So I continued. "And finally, while you might think that George believes you about not caring about Aaron, I can tell you were lying from the way you sobbed. That's not just a money thing."

She narrowed her eyes at me, and I braced myself for being all wrong about everything and getting clobbered by the beer bottle next to the leg of her chair.

Instead, she leaned back with her head tilted to the sky and watched the clouds skitter across the stark blue of a sunny day. How was it still just after noon?

"You know, I really did love Aaron—maybe not like I wanted to love someone, but he was good to me and we had flirted back in high school so long ago. Do you know what it's like to be put on a pedestal and made to feel that you can do no wrong after years of being treated like dirt?"

I didn't, but I certainly wasn't going to interrupt her story when she was obviously on a roll.

"I could do no wrong," she repeated as she rolled her head along the back of the chair to look at me. "No wrong. And whatever I asked for I got, not matter how big or how small. He helped with the restaurant when we were going through a bad time. He gave me money almost every week and was even helping me research how to do real dinner cruises. I want to expand from this little place by the sea, and he believed I could do anything and was willing to help me." She closed her eyes. "And then he decided that he didn't want to just date anymore but wanted to get married. And all of my dreams died. Now with Leo's death things are going to be even worse. Aaron is a good guy who deserves better. He deserves better than me." And she cried again.

I wasn't sure what to do to help her. I hadn't ever been so mistreated that I'd rather be with someone I kind of liked than hold out for someone who I could actually love. And maybe she would have loved him one day, but it was apparent that it was more about what he could do for her and how he made her feel than it was about who he was as a person.

And because of all of that I couldn't imagine she would have turned him away unless she was playing me big time and I just couldn't tell. But those tears looked genuine. Things didn't make sense, though. If she was willing to play him, then what was the big deal about taking a ring, promising to marry, and then never actually going through with it? It wasn't like she hadn't been playing him this whole time anyway. Something to think about later. Now I needed to get more answers and then leave as soon as possible.

"Do you have any idea who would have wanted Leo dead, then? Because I have a few people I want to look into but it's more like scattershot than actual leads, and I have until tomorrow to figure this one out."

"Why tomorrow?" She sniffled and wiped her nose with her hand. Okay, no handshaking when this interview was done.

"Because tomorrow they declare it a suicide."

That sent her on another crying jag. At this rate I was going to be here all day with no new information other than that she was far more self-centered than I had previously believed.

"I don't know who would have wanted him dead. I wish I did because I'd go take them out myself. This is killing my niece, Janina. But as far as I know everyone liked him—even some of the people from my family."

"Well, that's interesting. So far all I've heard is that everyone hated everyone and there was no in-between."

She squinted at me. "That's not entirely true. There were several people who weren't letting the ridiculousness of some hundred-year-old feud get in the way of talking to one another. We're not exactly a big island, as you know. And if you cut out a whole part of the population because of their last name then you end up with not too many friends or colleagues."

That was certainly true. "I thought this just recently popped up again because I honestly had never heard of it before."

"You wouldn't have, it's only something that goes around in the inner circles. It wasn't brought out into the open until Leo's death. Everyone wants to blame everyone else and yet no one really knows what the heck is going on."

"So you have no idea who might have wanted Leo gone? No person in your family who knew about the impending marriage and wanted to stop it? Even someone who was in love with Janina and thought that Leo wasn't good enough for her? Maybe they warned her away from him and when she didn't stop they decided to take matters into their own hands, as it were?"

She looked up into the sky for a moment, shaking her head. With her gaze back on me she shook her head again. "I don't know anyone and I can't tell you who would have done something like this. It's totally against everything I thought Leo was."

"Okay." I got up and dusted my hands off. "Well, if you think of anything, please don't hesitate to let me know."

"Shouldn't I just tell the police?"

"The chief of police is the one who wants this ruled a suicide more than anyone else, so I have a feeling that, even if you went to him about something you thought of, it would get buried."

The frown on her face told me I might have gone too far, especially since as an Ahern she would be related to Barney Warrington. I quickly ran through the family tree in my mind and came up with the fact that Barney would be her uncle. Dang it. I swallowed and waited nervously.

"I'll give it some thought. Let me know what your grandmother says about the cruise dinner for tomorrow night. I can't do it tonight but I'll start prep." And with that I was dismissed. She got up from her patio chair and took herself inside without even saying goodbye.

Now what? I wasn't sure where to go or what to do. Manny was pretty much off the list because I believed he wouldn't have killed his best friend's nephew. And Sylvie was off the list too. I highly doubted she had been the one to kill someone who her niece loved, especially when she had completely benefited from his uncle. However, that money train was no longer coming in. Did Sylvie know that and killed Aaron's nephew because he'd cut off her money? That seemed a little extreme, but I wasn't ruling it out entirely just yet.

So I had a jilted lover who didn't really want to be a lover, just a money receiver. And her niece, who had supposedly loved this guy despite everyone hammering her about her choices.

And then there was Aaron. How was he taking this? I really needed to make time to catch him and Janina.

My phone started buzzing with incoming texts from Nick that he was finding nothing. But he was still out there at least.

I walked around the corner from the back of the restaurant with my head down and my thoughts running amok. So I wasn't overly surprised when I ran right into a body.

Chapter 16

Fortunately, this one wasn't dead, just very angry. On second thought, that wasn't a whole lot better.

"Why don't you watch where you're going?"

"I'm so sorry . . ." I let the rest trail off because I was face-to-face with Barney Warrington.

"Ah, our intrepid little investigator. I heard what you're doing. What do you have to say for yourself?" He was a big, blocky guy with a full military cut. His red hair was just a small blush on his head on the side, and it currently matched his red face.

"Well, I'd say 'excuse me,' except I think you're the one who ran into me." Fisting my hands on my hips, I stared him down. Or at least I attempted to since he was almost a foot taller than me. Fortunately it was still early afternoon and there were tons of people on the streets. Therefore no way for him to do anything to me without drawing a lot of attention.

"I didn't walk into you. You should watch where you're going. It might get you into trouble if you're not careful."

"Is that a threat?" Digging my hands into my pockets, I tried not to show that I was shaking, just a little.

"Not a threat at all. Why would I threaten one of Avalon's

finest citizens? I just don't want you to get yourself hurt." His voice had menace practically oozing from every word. "However, you might want to reconsider this career change you seem to have made. You know nothing about Leo. You have no idea what you're getting yourself into."

Well, wasn't that just a crock of bull? "I'm trying to make sure you don't railroad an investigation that doesn't appear to be happening at all just so that your family can save face." Oops, I said that out loud when I really shouldn't have.

His face turned redder. I hadn't thought it was possible, but it did. After a few breaths, deep ones, he ran his hand over his short hair and clenched his fist at his side. "You're a fool. I'm trying to save you from yourself, but if you don't step back you might be the next one on the slab right next to Leo. Don't try to save the reputation of someone who didn't even deserve to be dunked in the ocean if he was on fire."

With that he turned away and stalked off down the street. A couple of kids were yelling at each other across the street to the beach, and I had a feeling they were about to get far more attention than they normally would.

Barney had been angry, really angry. And not necessarily only about me looking into things, but that I could get myself hurt. Was that real, or was he just trying to scare me so I wouldn't look into things more?

And what did he mean about Leo not being who I thought he was? I'd known him for years. My family had known his for even longer. It was just him being a pill and not wanting me to look into things. My gut wasn't completely on board with that. I ignored it this time.

I pushed the whole episode aside and went to look for Goldy and then call Maribel before heading to see Jake Ahern's mother. Maribel and I had things to discuss and I had to get an answer back to Sylvie as soon as possible, plus stop Goldy from inviting everyone tonight.

Who knew life could be so busy? All I had wanted to do was run a shop on a quiet island and have casual interaction with the locals and the tourists. Instead, I was running around like that proverbial chicken. Now I just had to make sure I didn't get my head cut off.

I found Goldy right where I thought she'd be, in my shop selling more of her rocks.

When the last customer stepped out of the store, happily ready to lay down their purchase on some unsuspecting road, I cornered her.

"Where are you getting all these rocks and how on earth are you getting people to buy them? We've sold more rocks in the last two days than I've sold all other merchandise in the last two weeks."

"I'm making some myself and getting people in who want to paint their own. You're not going to complain about the extra money coming in, are you?" Goldy had one of the scarves from the wall wrapped around her throat and thrown over her shoulder. I wondered if those were going like hotcakes too.

I stood there for a moment, debating with myself. I couldn't be angry about the shop making money because that would be stupid. And I couldn't be mad that Goldy had come up with something that had people coming back to get more and therefore keeping my shop afloat.

I guess I could have been mad about the fact that she came up with it instead of me, but that sounded stupid, even in my own head.

"Not mad." I looked at the floor and huffed out a breath. "Maybe I should just leave it all up to you, and I'll fill in shifts where I can."

She burst out laughing. "You are not getting out of this that easily."

My eyes snapped up to meet hers. "What do you mean? I'm

not trying to get out of anything. I just realize that you're a whole lot better at this than I am, so why continue to torture myself?" My words brought up the conversation I'd overheard between Sylvie and George about her torturing herself. What had she meant by that?

"You know, sometimes it does take a team, honey. You're far better at managing the books and keeping track of inventory than I am. And making business decisions. Lordy, there were so many things I wanted to do with the boat before your grandfather convinced me we should retire from the tours, and I was thankful once I saw how disastrous it could have been. So I'm good at one part, but you're better at the other. Together we could work on this."

That last part almost sounded like a question. When I looked up at her again, she was smiling a smile that was edged around the corners with uncertainty. Did she really think I'd kick her out and tell her I couldn't work with her just because she was better at something? I had been more willing to step out myself.

"We could." I eyed her as she stood there and a memory popped into my head of her and my father, her son. He'd been working on starting a boat-cleaning business and had wanted the reins completely to himself. I was too young to understand what exactly that meant, but they'd had a huge fight where I'd run to my room crying. I could still hear them, though, and my grandmother asking him to bend, just a little, and let them help so that he wouldn't have to stress so much. He didn't, he wouldn't, maybe he couldn't. And then he and my mother had left on their sailing trip and never come back.

Goldy's smile lost its uncertainty and beamed from her face. "If you're sure. I don't want to go all whale on you and have you feel like I'm taking over. I know I kid about that, but it really is a concern."

I could tell from the way she kept rotating her wedding band on her finger. Another memory popped, this one of my mother and Goldy going at it because Goldy thought that my mother wasn't spending enough time with us kids and that when she was with us she might want to play with us, hug us, or interact with us instead of always being on the phone with her friends or out shopping. I remembered trying to climb into my mother's lap and her shoving me back to the floor and saying she needed new shoes.

Where were all these memories coming from? I hadn't thought of my parents in years, had said goodbye to them in my mind almost as long ago. I'd always thought that at least they'd left us with people who cared about us.

And Goldy and Pops had. More than any other child could hope for without smothering. If she wanted in on this opportunity, I could do that and not feel so alone, not deal with the uncertainty all by myself.

"We can," I said with more force behind it. "You come in whenever you're available and we'll make a schedule of other times if I need off or you do. With Pops back manning the *Bounder* with Nick, I don't see why you have to stay home and stare at your fingernails all day. Besides, at least you won't be able to take in as much sun and maybe you won't get skin cancer. I'll save you from using too much Hawaiian Tropic."

The look on her face was one I'd only seen when I had gotten off the Catalina Express ferry that last time with all my worldly possessions with me. Like coming home, like I'd returned and that made her feel settled.

Of course she'd immediately gone back to being bossy, and she probably would this time too, but I could deal with that.

"So where does this leave us on the consignment thing?" She fingered the silk piping on her bathing suit cover.

"That's up to you. I'm willing to go all in, considering how well these things are selling. We can go over the books together, and I'll bore you to death with inventory, and then we'll both dive into making this place a thriving hub." Or at least I hoped that was what would happen. We had time and, with her savvy and expertise, we might not have to worry about it anyway.

"You're sure you don't mind me horning in on things?"

I took the hand that was still fiddling with the piping and brought it to my cheek. "I'm absolutely sure, Goldy. This is going to be fun and with the four of us working together I'm sure we'll be that much stronger, not to mention we can all have our own outside interests if no one is going it alone. I know how much Nick appreciated Pops coming out of retirement to run the boat so he can fly. I'd like to explore more things around the island again, and having Felix here means I would get to spend more time with him."

"Well, there is that . . ." she said. "And maybe with extra time you could get a move on with those wedding plans and great-grandchildren?"

I laughed as I stepped back from her. "That I'm not so certain of. Now, let's get to work. We need to move the food cruise to tomorrow night because Sylvie can't possibly have everything ready by tonight."

Goldy nodded. "I was wondering about that. I haven't invited anyone yet, so we're good there."

That was easy enough, thank goodness. I walked to the open front door, ready to leave. "So my next order of business is that I really need to talk with Janina. Do we know anyone who knows where she might be?"

I didn't have to call anyone or look too far, because at that moment she jogged past my front door looking over her shoulder—and ran smack into the sidewalk sign Goldy must have placed out there this morning that said something about getting your rocks off.

Janina stumbled and would have met the pavement with her face if I hadn't grabbed her in mid-fall. Once she was standing on her own two feet, I looked into her frightened eyes and pulled her into the store, shutting the door behind me and flipping the sign to CLOSED.

"What's happening?"

"Oh, God, can you please hide me? I don't think they saw me come in here, and I just can't face anyone right now, and most definitely not them. Please. Do you have a back room or something? Somewhere I can just sit and think about everything before facing anyone else?"

"Of course," I said with no hesitation at all.

Goldy opened the back room door and I ushered Janina in. I whispered for Goldy to open the store back up so no one would think anything was amiss as I grabbed a bottle of water from my mini fridge. I handed the water to the obviously shaken Janina in order to give her a moment.

She looked like she'd run a twenty-two-mile marathon when that would be impossible around here without doubling back over yourself.

Her hair was damp, her T-shirt had streaks of sweat on it, and her eyes looked bloodshot.

Basically a mess. While I wouldn't have been surprised seeing her as an emotional mess, this physical mess was far more worrying.

"What on earth is going on? I was just going to try to find you and here you are, which I'm thankful for, but why are you in such bad shape?"

"I need help, Whit. A lot of help, and I don't have anyone to turn to." She tried to take a deep breath, but it seemed to hitch in her throat.

Putting my hand on her shoulder, I grabbed my emergency bag of chocolate from the corner of the desk and opened it for her. "Just sit for a minute and calm down. You're not going anywhere, and I won't let anyone take you."

I didn't know if I could actually deliver on that promise, especially if it was the police who were chasing her, but just the thought of being safer seemed to bring her breathing more under control. So we'd ride that story out until it came to a sticking point.

My phone pinged with a text. I grabbed it out of my back pocket to see who needed me.

DO NOT MAKE A SOUND IN THERE. EXPLAIN LATER.

It was from Goldy. I didn't want to panic Janina even more, so I smiled as I typed back my thanks and then put my phone back into my pocket.

"Now, are you better?" I asked softly, and handed her a few paper towels from the dispenser in the bathroom off the office, then picked up a folding chair and quietly set it down so I could sit across from her.

"Do you have tissues? I don't know if I can blow my nose with these after all the crying I've done since Leo was found dead Wednesday." She handed back the paper towels, pushing them toward me like they burned her hands.

"Sure."

Getting up from my chair, I reached around her to the desk drawer where I kept the tissues. Opening it almost made me gag.

"What the heck?" I said.

"Why does your drawer smell like that horseback riding place in Middle Ranch?" Janina said and gagged herself as the smell of horse manure permeated the room.

Chapter 17

Why *did* my drawer smell like horse manure? Did someone break in and put a patty in here to warn me off like the rock was supposed to?

But that thought reminded me that I had put the rock in here with the tissues as a safe place to keep it but not have to look at it. Gingerly, I took the thing out of the drawer. The smell got worse. And then I realized: what I'd thought was black paint was actually horse poop.

Seriously unpleasant, but who was up on Middle Ranch that would want to give this to me? In all the other stuff going on I had completely forgotten about the rock and the warning message.

"Gag! What is that and why do you keep it in a drawer?"

I admit that Janina didn't know me very well, so she had every right to think that I might actually want something like this in my drawer. The problem was coming up with an answer that wouldn't scare her away before she answered my questions.

Since lying still wasn't my strong suit, I decided to go with the truth. If I expected her to be honest with me, it might go a long way toward that happening if I was honest with her first.

"Someone put it on my golf cart seat after Leo was found

and I was asked by his family to look into why he was killed. They don't believe he would have killed himself. Do you believe it was suicide?"

I didn't try to keep eye contact with her when I asked, since this was going to be a painful conversation for her, no matter how it came about.

"Absolutely not, and my aunt is not happy about it, and neither is my uncle. They both think I'm just making trouble and should admit that I know it is, and let my family do their job. 'Put this all behind us,' in their words." She snorted in disgust and wrapped her arms around herself. Like she was trying to hold all the broken pieces together. I knew that feeling.

I lightly touched her hand where it clamped on her elbow. "Hey, this is a no-judgment zone in here. Goldy could confirm that for you but I don't want to open the door to get her endorsement. I don't think he killed himself either."

She sniffed. "I can't believe anyone would be stupid enough to believe he had. And that suicide note they think they have is crap."

"How do you know? Have you seen it?" Man, I wished I could grab my notepad of all my questions and put checks next to the things she'd be able to answer for me.

"Because there was no reason for him to think that we weren't going to be together. That's what Fred keeps insisting it says, along with stupid Barney. I'm glad they are more distant relatives than my aunt. I don't think I'd want the genes that they must all be carrying."

I held in my giggle because it was incredibly inappropriate, but she looked much more belligerent now than sad. I wanted to keep her that way. "I know all about genetics and hoping you don't get a certain strain." Like the one that makes you leave your family and never come back even though yours kids might have needed you.

But this wasn't about me and my messed-up parents. This was about her and her messed-up family's insistence.

"So why are they so sure that he killed himself?"

"First, because they want to be, and second, because my aunt told them that I broke it off with Leo when she told me to. She's totally wrong on that account. In fact, Leo and I had plans to go to the mainland and just start over there together. We didn't have to stay here. We had other options. I wasn't going to let some stupid feud tell me what I could and couldn't do. But I told Aunt Sylvie what she wanted to hear from the beginning so that she'd get off my back and give me enough space to make plans to leave. Leo had it all figured out and his uncle was helping us get the right passes and set up an apartment in Long Beach." She started crying again, but I didn't try to stop her because she probably needed it this time.

I had a lot to think about, and had to figure out which question to ask next.

"So your aunt thought you'd broken it off with him and told the family as much. And then what? She thinks he killed himself because the two of you couldn't be together?" Like Romeo and Juliet without the fake-death thing beforehand.

"She can think whatever she wants. Aunt Sylvie and her ego are quite the pair, and she has no room to talk about anything. She was playing with fire and deserves whatever comes her way."

Banging on the door stopped my questions and made Janina and I look at each other. I was pretty sure there was as much fear in my eyes as I saw in hers. Had we made too much noise and someone had gotten past Goldy? Or had they hurt her to get past her?

More banging. "You'd better come out," a man insisted, "or I'm going to break down the door! You were told to get your butt home, or they were going to make sure you couldn't leave again!"

"That's one of the guys who works with my uncle," she whispered. "Please don't make me go with him," she begged.

"I won't." I pulled my cell phone out of my pocket and dialed the police. I wouldn't tell them what exactly was going on, but I would certainly say something to get them down here.

But before I could dial anything there was a kerfuffle outside. I heard the man yell in pain and then Pops yelled back that it was the least of his worries.

Scuffling ensued and I heard Felix's voice raised but couldn't understand the words.

A softer knock came through the wood and a text popped up on my phone:

COAST IS ALMOST CLEAR. GET READY TO HAVE A SERIOUS TALK ABOUT THAT BOYFRIEND OF YOURS. —POPS

Pops. For some reason he always had to sign his texts, like I couldn't tell from the sender on the texting program.

OPEN THE DOOR. —POPS

And so I did, to find myself walking into chaos. Parts of my store were almost destroyed, shelves broken and things lying on the ground, smashed and broken. I didn't take the time to be sad about that, though, because Felix was holding a bottle of water against his eye, Pops looked winded, and Goldy had a steaming mad going on. There was no one else in the store.

"Did he get away?" It was the first and only question I could come up with. Janina cowered behind me and had her hand fisted in the back of my T-shirt.

"Not without a lot of bruising and some blood, I'll tell you that." Pops looked like he was boasting and smiled broadly at Felix. "That boyfriend of yours has a serious right hook. I wouldn't want to get in a brawl with him unless it was the two of us against another person." He slapped my poor boyfriend on the back. Felix staggered to the side and caught himself on one of the broken shelves.

"Sorry, Whit. I'll come in with my tools tomorrow and get this all fixed back up." Felix took the bottle away from his eye and I could see a shiner was already starting to form. Poor guy.

"I can help him," Nick said as he walked in through the front door. "Heard about the commotion out on the street. Funny how fast this kind of thing can travel. Thought I should come down to check things out."

"Don't even worry about it. And if we can catch whoever did this, I guarantee you I'm not paying for anything to be fixed as it will be coming out of his bank account, not mine." I looked around again. "So who was it?"

"I honestly couldn't tell you," Goldy said, still mad as a lobster about to go on the boil.

"What? With all that commotion and him standing yelling at the door, you couldn't tell who he was? Did he have a mask on or something?"

"No mask, but I've never seen the man before and that's saying something. Do you think someone hired a bad man to come get Janina for some reason?"

We all looked at Janina but she was looking at the floor. "Was he wearing boots?" She squatted next to a particular mark on the floor and used a tissue to swipe at it, then brought it all up for us to see. "Horse manure, Whit. Horse manure, again. I think he's the one who gave you the rock. But why would someone from my uncle's ranch be trying to hurt me? I don't understand it."

"Me neither, sweetie, but we'll figure it out. Maybe we should go to the police station and file a report." I took the tissue from her and stuck it in a plastic bag. I didn't think it would necessarily prove anything but what did I know?

"We're coming to you," Deputy Ray Pablano said from the

doorway of my store. "We got a call about the disturbance from your neighbors next door."

So would this go well, or would Ray have been taken on board by the chief and told that, no matter what, he was not to talk to me because I was a nuisance and should keep myself safe?

Instead of spouting off about all the things that had happened recently, I stayed silent and waited for him to make the next move.

He didn't take long. "I need a description and a rundown of what happened. Then I need to know what you know about this suicide that's most definitely not a suicide. I did not move out here from San Diego to be told not to do my job because it's inconvenient for other people to have reality brought to their door."

I let out the breath I'd been holding. "Where do you want to start? Goldy can probably give you a description, but I can tell you he probably lives, works, or is visiting the Middle Ranch up in the hills. We have a manure sample, but it's not in any kind of uncontaminated container."

"You watch a lot of that television crime stuff?" he asked with his head cocked to the side.

I nodded and he sighed.

"Well, one point against you isn't the end of the world. Let's get down to business. Goldy, can you work with a sketch artist if I bring one into the store?"

She nodded too, and smiled.

"Felix, did you get a good look at the guy before he planted his fist in your face?" Ray turned toward Felix, who had put the bottle of water back on his eye.

"Yeah, I'd be able to identify him, and I have a piece of his shirt. I didn't just stand there while he was throwing punches, in case you were wondering."

"I would never wonder that," I said, standing at Felix's side.

"We know you put up a good fight. We should see the other guy, huh?"

Felix laughed, then winced. "Yeah, I'm sure the other guy isn't in much better condition at the moment."

"Did you see where he went?" Ray asked.

Felix gestured to the left and another deputy went out to look around.

"So with everyone here, let's get things started. I'm not taking anyone to the station to interview at the moment because I'm not sure what kind of reception you'd get there. But I will tell you that your aunt is looking for you, Janina. She's called four times in the last hour wondering where you are and wanting to report you as missing."

Janina looked baffled. "Why? I told her I was going for a walk. She should know exactly where I am. I've only been gone for, like, thirty minutes."

"Were you with her an hour ago?" I asked, thinking the timing was very off on this whole thing.

"No, I was at home, trying to make myself get ready for work. I told her I'd be in a little late because I just needed to sit with this by myself. She's been all over me about what happens with Leo's money and what he was doing before he hurt himself, and I just couldn't take it anymore."

She started pacing. I took the time to let my brain run over everything she'd said. Something wasn't connecting for me. I couldn't quite put my finger on it. If the aunt thought that they had truly broken up and that Leo had killed himself, then why would she wonder about the money? He was young enough that he probably had no will and his money would just go to his parents.

And why was the woman so worried about the girl when she had known where she was and where she was going? Janina had only been gone for thirty minutes—per her timekeeping—yet Sylvie had called the police four times over the last hour.

Unless Janina was the one lying and she was the one who had killed Leo? Maybe he hadn't really wanted to go off island with her and she had just made the story up to cover her tracks.

She did work at the golf course; Goldy had told me that. And I had smelled that floral scent under all the male cologne when I'd been at the scene of the crime Wednesday. Could she have killed him then hightailed it back to work as if nothing had happened? Maybe she had thought she'd get his money if she could say that they had still been together.

I doubted that would hold up in court against Leo's family. Especially if they hadn't wanted them to be together in the first place.

It was all a jumble up there in my brain, but I didn't know where to start.

Until Janina said, "Aunt Sylvie needs to get off my back and take her stupid husband with her."

Chapter 18

"Hold on," I said, trying desperately to get everything to sit right in my mind and not confuse myself. I didn't want to ask the wrong question that then would lead to the wrong path. "Did you just say Sylvie is married?"

"Pssh, yes, to some stupid jerk that only comes around at night after I'm supposedly asleep. They've been married for a while now, and I didn't even know about him until I kept smelling horse manure in the house and demanded to know what she was doing."

"But I thought she was dating Aaron Franklin." I didn't mean to blurt that out, especially with everyone standing in the room.

"What?" Janina yelled. "No way! She couldn't stand him and told me that nothing good ever came of hanging with a Franklin. That's why I could do so much better than Leo." She started tearing up again. "I couldn't, though. He was everything and he even gave my aunt money so that she could keep her place open. She wasn't using it right, though, and she deserves to have it taken away from her. That was money we were saving to get off the island and instead she bought new clothes and jewelry."

Now I knew for a fact that this was not the story Sylvie had told me. So which one was true? Who could I believe? And where did this all lead anyway? If Leo had been the one giving her money and she'd been taking it but told me she was getting it from Aaron, what was the purpose of that?

"And you don't know who she's married to?" I asked.

A shrug. "I really don't care. I just wanted to get off this island and start over with Leo, and now I have nothing. I don't even know what I want to do anymore, but I guess I can quit my job at the golf course now since I'm not saving up for a wedding anymore." One quick sob and then she wiped under her eyes. "Sorry. It's just a lot to process."

And I still wasn't sure who I believed.

I looked over at Ray. He was staring at the girl like he wasn't sure either. I considered asking him to talk with me in the back room to sort things out between us, but I didn't want to press my luck too far at the moment.

Ray shook his head and tucked his thumbs into his gun belt. "I think I need this to be more official than I had originally thought. I'm going to need you to come with me, Janina. We'll get you in an interview room to get some facts down and go from there."

For her part, Janina looked at me as if asking if I thought this was the best way to go about things. I honestly wasn't sure, but I had some things to look into before I knew whether I could trust her or not. And I figured that with her relatives at the station, and Ray questioning her, she'd at least be safe from whoever had tried to run her down and had her hiding in my store.

"Why don't you go with him, Janina? I'm sure we'll get to the bottom of all this. Then once we know what happened, we can hold the right people responsible."

Her nod held a world of hesitation, but finally she went with

Ray. He tipped the visor of his ball cap in my direction as they walked out the door, and I hoped I had not just handed her to the greater of two evils.

I went to Felix as soon as they were gone. "Are you going to be okay?"

"Yeah, I've had worse. Don't worry about me. What do we do next?" he asked. "I didn't get a bunch out of the golf game earlier today or the diving session, so I don't have anything to add at the moment."

I looked at Nick.

"Not much here either, sister dear. People just don't talk to me like they do to you."

I looked over at Pops and Goldy. "Can you guys stay with Felix until the sketch artist gets here? I have to go hunt down Aaron and hope that at least one person will tell me the actual truth. I'll take Nick with me for protection."

"Of course, honey." Pops slung an arm around Felix's shoulders. "You do have quite a right hook. Where'd you come up with that maneuver?"

Felix laughed weakly. "I didn't exactly grow up in the best of neighborhoods, sir."

"Oh, we can drop the formalities. You just took a shot for my granddaughter. I think it's time you call me Pops."

Goldy and I exchanged a glance. "Pops?" I said.

"Pops," she returned with a big old smile.

I'd deal with that later. Right now I had a very real need to speak with Aaron and find out what in the heck his side of the story was. Because if Sylvie had a husband, and Leo had been giving her money, then how did Aaron fit into all this? I was determined to find out, come hell or . . . well, I was already in the high water up to my nostrils.

I looked at the clock and was surprised to find it was almost

five. Where had the day gone? Right, to sleuthing my heart out.
As long as I got to keep my head I thought I might just be okay.

"Last I heard, Aaron was out with Manny, looking for birds."
Pops turned with his arm still around Felix's shoulders, and I
wasn't sure how far I wanted to go with that. I liked Felix as a
boyfriend, and I laughed at Goldy and her great-grandchildren
desires, but if they folded him into the family and then he decided to leave, how on earth were we going to survive that?

Again, something to put away and deal with later.

"Oh, hey, Goldy, before we get into all this other stuff, don't
forget that Sylvie had to move your dinner to tomorrow night—
if she's even going to be available after all this."

"I'm sure she'll figure something out to save herself. She always does."

We'd see about that.

After calling Jake Ahern and leaving a voice mail message to
let him know that any visit with his mom would have to wait, I
brought Nick up to speed. Just as I was getting to the end of
what I knew, Jake called back.

"No worries," Jake said sadly. "She took a turn for the worse
last night and they have her on a ventilator, so you'd have a hard
time talking to her anyway. I did ask a few questions, but she
kept talking as if she and my dad had just gotten married. I don't
think she'd have been helpful."

"I do appreciate you trying, Jake. We'll figure this out. Just
stay safe."

"You do the same."

We hung up and I looked at Nick. "Plan B."

Nick and I found our first bird-watcher at the beach. I hadn't
been able to get ahold of Aaron on his cell, so we thought hiking
around might be our only option.

Binoculars up, notebook at the ready, Thelma Freemont was intently looking out across the sea. From what I had heard she barely had any vision left and her glasses' prescription was so thick that she had to have a strap around the back of her head to keep them from sliding down her nose. But here she was, out on the beach, looking for that ever-elusive whatever the bird of the day was.

"Thelma," I said, approaching her from the left because that was the one good ear she still had. The other one she refused to wear a hearing aid in because according to her she wasn't old. Ninety-two looked good on her, after all.

"Shhh, shhh, I see a wingdingy and I'm not going to miss being able to say this one is all mine. Can't wait to wave that in Manny's face! Twitcher, my rear end. *I'm* the twitcher, I'll tell you!"

She hadn't even turned toward me so I waited as patiently as possible for at least two minutes. Okay, maybe it was more like thirty seconds, but I did stay quiet until she lowered her binoculars and stared at me, squinting.

"Marianna?" she said and I was quick to not fall over. Nick gripped my arm hard. That was my mother's name. I knew I looked like her but had never been mistaken for her.

"Uh, no, it's Whitney."

"Whitney?" She seemed confused for a moment and then clacked her false teeth together. "Yeah, yeah, Whitney. Marianna is gone, hasn't been seen in years. Whitney's the daughter, you old twit." She shook her head and then squinted at me again. "What do you need? I'm twitching."

"Okay, sorry. I was just wondering if you could tell me where Aaron is, or even Manny."

She snorted. "Up over at the golf course, trying to make a game plan to find out what happened to his nephew since you're taking too long."

It had barely been a little over twenty-four hours. I took a deep breath. "So they're over where Leo was found?"

"Yep, bad kid trying to make good, should've never gotten involved with those Aherns. They've never done anything right. Except turn their head when the Franklins were making their moonshine. Best and only good decision they ever made."

So it *had* been moonshine and the Aherns had known about it. As the police they should have put a stop to it and arrested people, but they'd probably taken a jar or two themselves back when all the states were dry.

I really wanted to explore this more, but I had to find Aaron.

"Poor Deli, never stood a chance against those yahoos. She never did drown, but then she shouldn't have said no to Chet if she wanted to live. My momma said that all she'd have to do is wait and he would have killed himself with drink anyway, but she didn't listen and then she drowned while drunk. Never drank a day in her life, poor girl."

I did sit in the sand for that one. Nick, not understanding the significance of what we were hearing, remained standing with a puzzled look on his face.

Who were Deli and Chet? Could this be the feud? Could Deli have been a Franklin who didn't want to marry Chet Ahern, so he'd gotten her drunk and then drowned her?

Where was my freaking notebook?

It was in my backpack so I grabbed it out and wrote everything down as a reminder to go back to the *Catalina Islander* archives. I remembered the name Delilah from one of the accident articles. Maybe they were one and the same.

"Thelma, do you know anything about the new murder?" It couldn't hurt to ask.

"I was out that day, looking for the ashy storm petrel Aaron was crowing about. I saw his golf cart but I didn't see him in it, and it sure did smell like flowers when I went to see if I could steal his notebook."

Smelled like flowers . . . the gardenias? Or Sylvie's Red Door perfume? So had she been the one to kill Leo, and she was trying to throw everyone off the scent by coming clean about some stuff but not others?

I really needed to talk to Aaron.

"Thelma, I have to go, but if you think of anything else you know where you can find me."

"Yep, down at the old drug store. I don't go there anymore, though, because what's the point, just a bunch of froufy stuff that's pointless. Now if you had some bird-watcher stuff I might just be in." She looked at me again through her glasses and winked. "See you later, toots. I got birds to watch."

I'd been dismissed by someone who might not know who I really was. But she seemed to have had answers I needed, and I hoped Aaron had the rest.

Nick and I took the autoette to the golf course and parked in the lot. I explained about the Ahern-Franklin feud on our way and told him to let me do the talking when we got to Aaron. I wasn't going to risk running into anyone I'd rather not see. Namely any Aherns.

We kept to the edge of the tree line as we made our way around the course to the eighteenth hole. There seemed to be some kind of parallel in Leo's life ending at the end of the course, but that could just be my mind trying to assimilate all the info I had floating around in there at the moment. I wouldn't put it past myself.

The sun was still relatively high in the sky when I looked at my watch. Almost dinnertime and I should be eating something yummy, maybe making plans for taking in a movie with Felix. Instead, I was on a golf course skulking around with my brother while Felix was probably getting fixed up at the urgent care.

Quite the life.

When we neared the last hole we slowed down to see if I could get any intel before busting in on a meeting I might not be welcome at. Three people stood facing Aaron. Was there hostility in the way they stood? Was this a fight that was about to break out? Or maybe they were plotting to kill someone again.

I wasn't leaving until I found out.

Chapter 19

"Look," Aaron said, "I know that I've made a mess of things, but I really need your help, everyone. I promise to stop lying about the birds I see if you just trust me on this. I need to know what happened to Leo and I need to know what happens next." That was definitely Aaron's voice. It had some gravel to it from being a big talker for years. Apparently he was being taken down a rung at the moment. Manny hadn't been that far off when he'd thought Aaron wasn't quite the twitcher he reported to be.

"I don't know, Aaron. If you lied in your book, then what's to say you aren't lying now?" That was definitely Manny. I peeked out around a tree and found myself feeling much like I had when I was spying on Sylvie. Hopefully I'd get information this way that I could use. Nick tried to peek over me and I shoved him back.

"I'm sorry. I know I shouldn't have lied, but I just wanted to fit in, and I never seemed to see anything but a sparrow or two. I swear to you that I'm not lying about this, though."

"I saw those tire tracks on the kid's chest, Aaron, and I know they match your tires. I was a mechanic back in the day and you always have wear on the one side because you don't rotate them like you should. So if you didn't run him over, then who did?"

Aaron folded his lips in and clasped his hands together in front of him. "I don't know!" he burst out. "I don't know. Someone is playing me. I can't help but think it's the Ahern family. Who else would do this to me and mine? Please help me. I promise I didn't run him over. When I went out in the morning to start bird-watching my cart was parked kind of funny in the garage, but I didn't pay any attention to it. I just thought maybe I had hit the mark wrong, but now I think someone might have moved it to use it to run Leo down and then didn't park it right when they brought it back."

Manny turned his back on his friend and paced away. "I'm still not sold. What's to say you didn't hurt him for dating that Ahern girl when he wouldn't leave her? Maybe you told him that he had to dump her, and when he told you no you decided to kill him to keep the family name intact."

And that was when Aaron started crying. Seriously, I had seen more tears in the last thirty-six hours than I had over the last three years. Were the tears because of Sylvie? Or from frustration?

I rushed out of the trees and put my arm around Aaron, Nick close on my heels. "Twitcher on not, you're mean, Manny. This man is your friend and deserves to be given some credit. So he lied about birding. He's not lying about this." Even though I'd only said Manny's name I looked around to make sure that Gerald McCormick and Ann Fritz—now that I recognized them—knew I was talking to them too about being mean.

Or at least I didn't think he was lying. Was I ready to put my life and reputation on the line for this guy if he was a liar? But I felt in my gut that while he might lie about what birds he saw, he would not lie about something this important.

"Oh, Whit, Leo's gone and I don't know if I'll ever be okay."

"It will never be okay," a female voice said from behind us.

We all turned to find Judith Franklin stepping out from the

trees. Leo's mom. Her eyes were bright red, her hair a mess, and her face so drawn she looked like a caricature.

Aaron stood for a moment, staring at her, then held his arm wide open when she rushed to him.

"Our baby's dead, and it will never be okay again."

"Oh, sweetheart. Whit's doing her best to figure things out. I told you to stay home. You don't need to be out here right now, not so soon after. Let us get him buried properly and then we'll put up a memorial. I promise." He kissed the top of her head while she bawled her eyes out.

I glanced over at Nick. "Can you take her home and make sure she gets there safely?" I asked him. "I need Aaron for a little while longer if I'm going to be able to figure out what happened to Leo."

Nick, bless his heart, did as I asked. I heard him murmur, "It's going to be okay. It's all going to be okay. Whit won't let you down," as he and Judith made their way back toward the golf course parking lot. I sincerely hoped he wasn't making promises I couldn't keep.

I turned back to the group of bird-watchers and noticed that Aaron's eyes never left Judith until after she rounded the bend with Nick.

"Okay, Aaron." I pulled him into a hug that he so obviously needed even if it wasn't really my arms he wanted around him. "I need you here with me. Nick is the best person to help her right now. As for your pain, it's going to be rough for a while, but it does get better." I held on to him for a moment longer, then set him away from me. "Aaron, I need you to tell me more about the golf cart. Who had access? Could they have hot-wired it? How secure is your garage?"

"My garage is secured by a lock. No one can get in unless they have the key, and no one but Leo had the key."

"So do you think Leo took the golf cart out and then someone ran over him and killed him, then brought it back to make it look like a suicide?" I was grasping at straws but they didn't seem so short on possibility at the moment.

"It's possible. But why would he take my cart out when he had his own? Unless he was going to meet that Janina girl. Sometimes he used my cart so that no one would realize it was him."

"Think about that for a moment. While you're doing that, I want you to tell me about your relationship with Sylvie."

He shot a startled look at me and took a step back while pulling me with him. "I can't do this here. No one knows about my relationship with Sylvie. It's over now anyway, so it doesn't matter. I'm already hurting, Whit, do we have to make this worse right now?"

Even though he looked ready to cry again, I couldn't save him from it this time. "You and I can talk privately if you want, but I was thinking of asking your friends to help with a scouting mission. First I need to know what your relationship was with her. They'll probably find it out anyway."

"No one did over the course of the last few months. I'm pretty sure it was a safe secret until I decided to go too big."

"What do you mean?"

"I wanted to make her my wife and she freaked out—but not in a good way. Then Leo died and she called it off altogether, saying that she wasn't willing to risk her life to be with me."

That was slightly different from the version she'd told me earlier, but it still left questions.

"Are you aware she's married, Aaron?"

"What?" he yelled. "Absolutely she is not married!"

We turned at the collective gasp behind us to find all of his bird-watching buddies leaning in to listen.

"Anybody need popcorn?" I asked.

Manny, of course, raised his hand, then put it down when I shot him a dirty look.

"You could be helping," I fumed at him with good reason. "You said he was like your brother. So he lied about some bird sightings. It doesn't change the fact that he's your friend beyond that, does it?"

Manny's scrunched-up face did not bode well for his answer being positive. "Well, that's a pretty important lie in my world, Whit."

There was some head nodding to accompany that statement, and it made me want to smack them all.

"You have got to be kidding me." I slapped my hand against my leg, hurting myself because I forgot I was wearing shorts. I ignored the pain and continued. "You mean to tell me that every single one of you has always been honest about every single bird you've ever seen?"

The nodding turned to awkward glances away, Manny included.

"And if you were in a bad position, and someone thought you had killed your nephew, then wouldn't you want your supposed friends to help you out in any way they could?" I gave each of them a few seconds of attention as I stared around the trio. I was not going to let them get off that easy.

"Please, guys," Aaron begged. "I don't know what else to do, but I know Leo wouldn't have killed himself, and I know I didn't do it. We have a murderer running loose on the island. If you won't do it for me, will you do it for Whit? I just need answers and then I promise I'll go away from all your lives. I'll even cross the street if I happen to be on the same sidewalk."

I looked around and expected a tough crowd from their earlier comments, but Manny was the only one who still appeared to have steel in his eyes.

Thelma came up behind him, joining our little birder society get-together, and knocked him in the shoulder and nudged him forward. "You go on and tell him that you'll help him. He deserves that. He tries hard and you're not much of a twitcher yourself, if you ask me. I think you just like an excuse to use those binoculars."

Manny's ears turned red and I could feel him weakening. Taking Aaron's hand in mine, I turned toward the whole crowd. "Even without Manny we can do something to help. Sylvie has a husband, according to her niece, and I'm told that he only visits at night because they don't live with each other. I need to know if he comes down from the Middle Ranch." That would answer so many questions—the smell of manure in the house, the person who left the "rock" on my golf cart seat.

It wouldn't tell me who killed Leo, but it could at least solve this one mystery and maybe lead to other questions I could ask to get down to the bottom of this whole thing.

"So what do you say?" I looked at the trio again and got nods from everyone, including Manny. But he kept his eyes down and his arms folded across his broad chest.

"This is what I need you to do, then. I need you out tonight, looking for anyone coming near Sylvie's house. Don't engage and certainly don't try to apprehend anyone, just watch and report in. Do you guys have each other's cell numbers? Can we station you along the road down from the ranch and then relay the info for whom to look at as he makes his way down? It won't be just us, we'll have additional help." It would be like lighting the beacons of Gondor from *The Lord of the Rings* and could go awry if someone got too zealous but at this point I had few options and less time. Had I just done a horrible thing? I tried not to believe so as we walked back to the parking lot and the four birders separated to reach their vehicles. Aaron was the last to get into his golf cart. He had been left behind as the other three walked together, chattering excitedly and trying to come up with a viable story as to why they were out at night.

They'd come up with bats, even though they weren't birds, and maybe some owls. All without a single word from Aaron.

I rushed to catch up with him, but didn't need to, as he just sat in his cart with the ignition off and his hands on the wheel. His head was dropped down so far his chin touched his bony chest.

"Aaron?"

He looked up with red-rimmed eyes and so much sadness that I didn't know what to do for him except go stand near him and put my hand over his.

"We'll get to the bottom of this. I promise." I patted his hand.

"I'm already at rock bottom, Whit, and I don't know how much further I can possibly go." He clenched his fingers around the wheel and rolled his hands back and forth like he was riding a motorcycle. "I've lost my nephew, who I loved like my own child. I may have lost all my friends, and I guess the possible love of my life was so one-sided as to be funny. It's all a mess."

Maybe there was something I could do for him. "I know this isn't going to make things better really, but I can tell you that Sylvie did care for you. She might have a strange way of showing it, and leading you along while she was already married was a horrible thing to do, but when I talked to her about your relationship she was really broken up that it was going to end. She said you put her on a pedestal and treated her better than anyone ever had in her life. She was sad that it was over."

He blew out a breath. "I don't know whether to feel good about that or want to curse even more that I gave her everything and she was playing with me the whole time. What kind of person does that?"

"I have no idea what was going on in her head. I can't speak for her either, other than what she told me. You didn't know anything about her being married?" I had to know just in case he was the one playing all of us. But his dejection looked so totally genuine that I felt terrible for even asking.

"No, nothing. I would have never let her talk me into dating if I'd known. I should have never answered her phone call."

"Sylvie said the same thing, that she should have never answered your call and this would have all been okay."

"Bah! She's telling tales again. I didn't call her. We ran into each other at the post office, and she asked how I was doing. I told her just fine since that was the answer I wanted her to believe and tried to leave it at that. But she was adamant that we talk some more and invited me to coffee at her house. I put her off as long as I could, not wanting to get hurt again, but she was persistent. So I agreed to one coffee because I really did love her back in high school."

"That's understandable." I wouldn't have done it, but who was I to judge? Some things were much better left in the past.

"So we get to talking about life and she tells me that she's in a bad place. Not straight out of the gate, mind you, just a subtle hint here or there. And me being the idiot I am, I offered to help her financially. But she didn't want to anger her family so I sent the money to her through Leo's bank account since he was already dating her niece."

That explained how she could be in such dire straits at the restaurant but still offer free drinks. She was probably laundering the money through her bar so that it didn't look like she was taking money from anyone, least of all a Franklin.

"And then as soon as I wanted to take things to the next level she cut me off, and then Leo died, and now it's all gone to hell."

"Aaron, I'm so sorry. But we'll get this murderer, and while that won't fix everything, it will at least bring justice to your family."

"For the first time at least. And if those Aherns up at the sheriff's station think I'm taking this lying down like my great-

great-great-grandfather did, and falling in with an accident or a suicide, then they are sorely mistaken."

"What?" I held onto the railing of the cart at Aaron's eye level and leaned in. "What do you mean, like your great-great-great-grandfather?"

"That freaking feud that everyone's always going on about but doesn't know what the heck they're talking about. My great-aunt was asked to marry by one of those Aherns and when she turned him down he backhanded her into the sea and blamed it on accidental drowning due to her excessive drinking and not being a good swimmer. But that lady had been a champion swimmer, swam around the whole island once, and she'd never touched a drop of that rot-gut moonshine Chet Ahern had wanted the recipe so bad for. He thought he'd marry her and get the rights to it but she said no, as was her choice. And when the cops were called to fish her out of the water, they said it was an accident without even investigating. Said they refused to prosecute one of their own, especially since my family wouldn't give them more money to keep hush about the illegal alcohol."

Delilah Franklin.

And there it was, the whole feud laid out at my feet. Right into my waiting hands. I could tell Reese back at the newspaper that I knew all the details now and why it was so horrible. And if we could get this solved and force Barney's hand, maybe we could have the investigation reopened. I didn't know if it would bring Aaron comfort, and I certainly wasn't going to offer him anything at the moment, but I might just know someone in place to open a cold case back up.

"Let's get through this and find out who killed Leo and why, and then we'll go from there."

"Yeah, I want my nephew's killer found, and I want it as soon as possible. Sylvie can hie off to whatever rock she climbed out from under a few months ago. If her restaurant fails, then that's on her." He turned the key in the ignition on his golf cart. "I think it would be better if you kept in contact with everyone this evening instead of me. I'll be out looking around, but I'll just wait to hear from you on how things are going—unless I spot the guy."

"I can take that for you, Aaron. We will get to the bottom of this."

"I'm already at my own bottom, girl. This can't get much worse."

He drove off as I stood in the parking lot for another moment, wondering how this all fit together and why someone would have killed Leo. Could it have been that they found out about the money and didn't want an Ahern taking money from a Franklin so they killed him? But that seemed so overboard.

Was it because they didn't want him dating one of their own? That also seemed overboard, but I didn't have too many other theories.

Hopefully someone would see a stealthy husband tonight and give us some answers.

Chapter 20

Three hours later, the battery on my phone was dying from how often this group I'd assembled texted one another. Every time something moved they had to report it and make sure to tell everyone that they were still on the lookout.

It was eleven o'clock at night and I was about to call it done. Maybe the guy didn't visit Sylvie every night. Maybe this was an off night, which meant I'd have to endure this whole thing all over again tomorrow.

But tomorrow I had an impromptu dinner cruise and the coroner would have already ruled Leo's death a suicide. That didn't sit well with me, so I continued to monitor the chatter.

WHERE ARE YOU, AARON? Manny texted.

ROAD TO MIDDLE RANCH, Aaron texted back. When I had tried to tell Manny, Gerald, and Ann that Aaron wanted me to handle everything, I'd gotten some serious pushback. It turned out they did want to help their friend, and he was not going to be able to bail out and leave the communication to me.

YOU SEE ANYBODY COME DOWN? I GOT A GUY WHOS AROUND YOUR HOUSE

Ah, the wonders of people not using punctuation in texts . . .

WHO

IDK SOME GUY

WHATS HAPPENING

Manny didn't automatically respond, and when he didn't Aaron texted again. Still nothing.

GOING TO CHECK, Aaron texted. I wanted to tell him to stay put but figured that was futile. From my vantage point at the park bench outside the restaurant with Whiskers at my side, there wasn't much I could do. If someone came down from Middle Ranch it would make sense for them to go by Aaron's house, but not to linger. Yet how had Aaron missed him on his way down the road? I would have thought he of all people wouldn't have been distracted even if an ashy whatever showed up and perched on his head.

Five minutes later, I got another text:

NEED HELP NOW

I didn't wait for anyone else to respond. I called Aaron directly, but he let the call go to voice mail. I called Felix, who was stationed at the Catalina Casino, and told him to get to Aaron's now.

We all converged at the same time to find Manny on the ground, holding his bleeding head, Aaron flapping his hands over him like wind could help, and Aaron's garage door dented and cracked right about at head height.

"Do we need an ambulance?" I asked first.

"No, it's just a cut and my bruised ego," Manny answered. He got up from the ground and staggered for a second until Aaron got his shoulder under him. Thankfully, Manny didn't shake him off.

"What happened?" Felix got to the question before I did.

"Some guy was checking out Aaron's garage, and I wanted

to see what he was doing. The binoculars weren't helping, so I came down and got smashed into the garage for my trouble."

Thelma came zipping up in her golf cart, followed closely by the other two birders. "What on earth? Are you okay?" She toddled over to Manny and I closed my eyes. No one was watching for the guy supposedly coming down from Middle Ranch, and now Manny was hurt. We wouldn't be able to identify the mystery man or even know if it was him in the first place. Maybe it had just been someone trying to burglarize the neighborhood.

Plus, with all of us gathered here it would be hard to miss that we all seemed to be in on some kind of mission. So to top it all off, we'd blown our cover with nothing to show for it.

"Manny, you really need to get to the urgent care at least and have that looked at," I said. "Did you see anything before you got clocked?"

"Not really. But I did bang his head pretty hard with my binoculars. Hard enough to make him drop his cigarette." He gestured toward the ground and sure enough there was a cigarette on the ground. It had gone out but I still was careful approaching it.

"We need to call this in to the police. At the least it's an assault and they need to look into it."

"They're already on their way," Thelma said.

Nodding at her for taking the lead on that one, I then bent over and got a whiff of the scent. I had never been a huge fan of cigarettes but this one had a particularly distinct smell.

A siren interrupted my perusal and it was all I could do not to scoop the cigarette up and take it home to give it some more thought. But that would be stupid because the cops would need it. As long it wasn't Barney, of course, or any other Ahern with Aaron standing here.

"Trouble?" Ray Pablano asked, stepping out of his vehicle with a resigned look on his face.

"Are you asking me, or telling me that's what I am?" I shot back and then wished I hadn't.

"Not telling you anything, Whit. I'll talk with the victim and then get him to the hospital. The rest of you might want to head on home before anything else happens."

I couldn't tell if that was a threat or a warning. Was Ray in Barney's pocket now? I hadn't thought so before when he'd been quick to take all those Aherns in at the golf course. But after questioning Janina this afternoon that could have changed, and I didn't want to be caught off guard.

"Thanks, Ray. Guys, I think the bat-watching is over for the night anyway. Thanks for all you taught me. I look forward to watching with you again." I gave the biggest smile I could muster through my frustration and then turned to Felix. "Since I walked, do you mind taking me home?" I asked, pointing to his autoette.

"Not at all. Jump in." He exchanged a look with Ray that I couldn't quite decipher. I blamed it on being tired and the fact that nothing was working out as I'd planned. Not to mention we still had the coroner coming tomorrow. If things didn't start moving along soon this was going to go down as a closed case of suicide.

I had to think of something else and I had to do it quick.

I had Felix take the backstreets-way home just in case we could catch a glimpse of a lone man walking around, holding his head after being hit with a heavy-duty set of binoculars. We saw nothing. Not even when we went by Sylvie's house. All the lights were out and the house silent.

"Damn. I really wanted to find out what was going on. And why was the guy checking out Aaron's garage? Do you think he was the one who stole Aaron's golf cart and then ran over poor Leo?"

"I have no idea," Felix answered. "And I'm starting to think that maybe we should let Ray handle all of this. Things are getting a little dangerous for my taste, and I don't want to see you hurt."

"Believe me, I don't want to get hurt either." I let the light evening breeze ruffle through my hair as I closed my eyes. "I don't want to get hurt, but so many other people are getting hurt, or will be hurt, if this murderer isn't caught. I just can't let him get away with it. What else do you propose I do?"

"I told you, let Ray handle it." He took a gentle turn to the right and I let my head roll in his direction.

"And you really think he's going to? Maribel said that they're not allowed to say anything but suicide, and tonight certainly didn't give him any new leads on making it anything but that. If they can't get it right from the beginning, then how are they going to make it right at the end?"

"I don't know, Whit, but I just feel like there's a lot going on under the surface that we don't know about. More than anything I want you safe."

"Like I said, I want to be safe too, but what about everyone else? Someone who's gotten away with murder might not hesitate to try it again since they did such a good job this time. Who's next?"

We pulled up in front of my house to find Maribel out on the sidewalk, waving her cell phone around madly.

"Don't you ever answer your phone? What the hell is wrong with you? I have news!"

Jumping out of the cart, I pulled my cell phone from my back pocket and realized I must have silenced it after all the chatter leading up to Ray's arrival on the scene.

"Sorry. What do you have?"

"Not out here." She looked left and right and then left again. "Quick, get inside. There's something I have to show you."

That had me double-stepping it into my rented house with Felix right on my heels.

"What did you find?" I asked after I slammed the door behind me. I'd almost clipped Felix, but he'd jumped out of the way fast enough to not get caught in my enthusiasm.

"Remember how you wanted to know who Sylvie was married to and why she'd hide him or where she'd hide him?" Maribel's face beamed like a thousand lights caught behind glass. She clasped her hands in front of her chest and seemed ready to burst with glee.

"Well, are you going to tell us, or do you think you'll pass out from holding your breath in anticipation of your reveal first?" I asked. "I did find out that Middle Ranch plays into this somehow, but I want to know how."

"Sorry, I'm so sorry. I'm just so excited about this and really hope it answers more questions than it makes, and I just wanted to tell you, but then I couldn't get a hold of you, and I wasn't sure where you had considered going bird-watching, so I couldn't even come look for you—"

"Maribel, please don't do this right now. Just tell me what you know!" I didn't mean to yell, and Whiskers was the first one to let me know it was inappropriate by swiping at my face. I dropped her on to the couch and grabbed Maribel by the elbows. "Take a deep breath and tell us."

She did just that. "His name is Raul and he works at the Middle Ranch. He's been there for several years about as long as they've been married. It looks like he might have come over on a vacation and never left."

"Do you have pictures? Is it someone we know?" I was racking my brain for people I knew who were named Raul, but the only one I could think of was almost a hundred years old. I was pretty sure he wasn't skulking over to Sylvie's nightly for a little loving.

But then I remembered the phone number that Pops had been given to call once he'd buried that treasure chest. That had been a Raul also. Was it the same person, though?

The Middle Ranch was a horse ranch up in the, you guessed it, middle of the island, on Middle Ranch Road. I hadn't been up there in years and definitely not since I'd moved back. But it was a shared stable for people who had horses on the island and for tourists who wanted to ride the trails in the area on horseback. It wasn't inexpensive but I remember it being wonderful when I went there as a child.

So why was he living there and Sylvie was living in town? If they had married several years ago, why didn't she immediately tell everyone? Unless he was another Franklin . . .

"What's his last name?" I asked.

"It's not Franklin, if that's what you were getting after. I looked. It's Martinez. I don't know any Martinez, and I really wasn't able to tell where he came from before now. I haven't taken the tracing course yet, and regular old internet search words have found nothing on him at all."

So close! "That's okay. At least we have a name now. Potentially, we could go up to Middle Ranch tomorrow and ask around about him. Maybe he's a trainer or a trail header. We could see about going out on the trail with him and getting him to talk. Or even offering to muck out a stall to talk."

"Uh, yeah." Felix laughed. "You can volunteer for any of those. I'm more of a hiking and swimming kind of guy, and I don't do mucking."

I looked over to Maribel.

"I have to be there for the coroner tomorrow. I thought maybe I could try to talk to him about having an open mind before Barney gets his claws into him."

I sighed. "All right. Well, that might work as long as he's not an Ahern."

"He's not," she said. "I looked that up too."

"Okay, so we have a name and the confirmation of a place, and now we just need to figure out motive. Opportunity would be nice too, but we really need motive more than anything, or we'll never get any further, and this Raul could be getting away with murder." I sighed. "But right now it's really late and I've been running after people for what feels like days. Let's sleep on it and go full force tomorrow."

There was general agreement from the other two, thankfully.

Felix kissed me goodbye at the front door and then Maribel and I said our good nights and headed to our bedrooms. It had been an incredibly long day with a lot of information to process and file away while trying to connect the dots.

I took out my notepad as Whiskers crawled into my lap and refused to let me write. Raising my knees, I left her in the valley of my lap and wrote on top of my knees.

We had intrigue and unknown people, golf carts stolen then put back, a woman who had thought it was fine to lead someone on as long as they didn't try to step out of line with what she wanted, an answer to the feud, and more questions than I could put to paper.

The biggest one I wanted to know was, who had killed Leo and what were they doing at this moment? How could I catch him or her and bring them to justice?

I went to sleep thinking about those things and woke up not sure what day of the week it was.

Ah, Friday, the beginning of most weekenders' vacations, a normally good day for the store, an influx of people. Oh, and it was the day the coroner was coming to declare Leo's death a suicide, and I had Goldy's dinner cruise lined up for tonight. What had I been thinking?

Since Felix didn't have any diving lessons this morning, I texted him and asked him to go looking into the Middle Ranch thing and take my brother with him. He tried to balk, but I was not taking no for an answer. I knew for certain that he wasn't going to have to muck any stalls, and he was a good guy to ask the questions I might get the side eye for.

Two minutes later, he texted back one word: FINE

Okay by me!

I finally rolled out of bed and tried to organize my day in my head. I had things to look into, but I also had to work at my store. I couldn't expect Goldy to not take things over if I never showed up to work again. Plus, we had to talk about the cruise and I had some ideas about who to invite.

And I wanted to try to talk with Janina one more time, to ask why she'd thought Leo was giving her aunt the money when it was really Aaron.

So much to do, and it wasn't going to get done by sitting around in my pajamas and eating dry cereal.

I fed Whiskers and gave her one last pat after I'd gotten myself dressed and ready for the day. I had a mission and I was not going to be stopped.

Except that when I went out to my golf cart, I saw the tires had been removed and someone had written a very nasty phrase across my windshield. One that told me very clearly where my questions and I could go.

Okay then, plan B. Thankfully everything around here was within walking distance, and I could always borrow a cart from the golf course if I needed to. We had places that rented them by the hour, but I didn't want to pay for it. Especially because I wasn't sure how long I was going to need it for.

I texted Maribel to see if she had seen the missing tires when she'd left this morning. She texted back that everything had seemed fine, but that Barney had moved her on to filing, and she wouldn't be able to catch the coroner so I'd have to think of another way to convince the good doctor to not listen to the station commander. Great.

Not sure where else to turn, I caught Felix on the phone before he left for Middle Ranch and asked him for a quick ride to the golf course.

"It's always something with you, isn't it?" he asked when he arrived, but then he kissed me on the cheek and laughed. "What do you think happened to your tires?"

"I'm sure they'll come back after I solve this whole thing, and quite frankly, right now I don't have time to deal with it. I will not be distracted today, so no points for the idiot who did that. I did take the time to clean my windshield, though."

"Good for you. So on to the golf course?"

"Yes, please, sir, and step on it."

Pulling away from the curb, he aimed for the golf course. It wasn't a far drive. Heck, I probably could have just walked it. But I was feeling like I would need the majority of my energy for my brain today. Exercise could happen tomorrow.

"Do you know what you're going to do first?" He turned to me when he pulled into the parking lot.

"I'm hoping to catch Janina here this morning. I need to ask her what she knows about the money her aunt was getting from Leo, and why he didn't tell her it was actually from his uncle. Then I'm going to go to Aaron's and see if he has any new information. After that I'll check on Manny before trying to meet the coroner before he makes it to the station, because Maribel got reassigned and won't be meeting him per Barney's orders. I'd like to smack Barney in the head for his underhandedness, but first I need to bend the coroner's ear for just a moment before he walks into the den of stupid."

"Hey, I work there."

"Right, and so do many other smart people, but I'm afraid if I don't get to him first that Barney will do everything in his power to make sure that the coroner only hears his story. I just can't let that happen."

"Makes sense. Let me know if you need anything else and I'll let you know what I find out at the ranch. You owe me big for having to go up there."

I kissed him on the cheek. "Consider it an IOU. And you're taking my brother, so if there's any mucking to do just make Nick do it."

He was chuckling as he drove away, so my job there was done.

Walking on to the course, I took in the manicured lawn and the different holes set up. I had never completely understood the lure of smacking balls with a club, but I knew they did a hefty business here and only wished them the best. Maybe I should see if they'd allow me to put some flyers up for the Dame of the Sea, or even put some of my merchandise in a case at the front desk so people knew what was available. If I could afford whatever they'd charge for the placement.

There would be time for that later, though. I just hoped a bunch of people didn't choose to put their new rocks on the golf course and get me in trouble for vandalizing the perfectly put together course.

I stood at the front counter and waited for Bethany to answer my ding on the desk bell. I wanted to talk with Janina, but first I had to find out where she was and this was the fastest way to do that.

Looking out over the lawns, I watched golf carts trundle along with their four-packs of people; lots of golfers out this morning and many of them with caddies. But then I saw one cart zoom around the exterior of the course with just a single occupant. And the cart looked familiar.

What was Aaron doing back on the golf course? Unless he thought maybe he could gain golfing friends now that his birder friends were waffling.

I let my eyes follow the trek of the cart and was not overly surprised when I saw it head to the eighteenth hole. Maybe he was visiting the spot where this had all started to say goodbye to his nephew before the autopsy.

The person was wearing a caddy uniform, though, not Aaron's standard cardigan and collared shirt. I stepped up to the window to get a better look and realized it was a woman, but then Bethany cleared her throat.

"What can I do for you, Whit?" She was well put together, as everyone on the course was. I made a point not to look down at my hastily assembled outfit.

I resisted the urge to also look over my shoulder to find out what was going on behind me with Aaron's golf cart.

"Uh, I was wondering if Janina was in? I had told her I'd drop things off to her today and just thought I'd get it out of the way before I open the store."

"Right, well." She hit a few keys on the keyboard at her computer. "It looks like she should have been here twenty minutes ago but she messaged that she can't find her uniform so she's going to be a little late. That happened the other day too. Maybe we need to think about getting her an extra to leave here." She brushed her bangs off her forehead as if just remembering I was still standing there. "Anyway, she's not in right now. Do you want to drop off the stuff with me? I can keep it back behind the counter for her."

"No, that's okay. I'll stop by later."

"Suit yourself. It's not like I have anywhere else to go. Daddy won't let me."

I was not going to have a conversation with the young woman about not being a jerk about her father footing everything from salon bills to housing to providing a job for his daughter where all she had to do was stand around and smile. Especially not when I had the eighteenth hole to check out and the need to figure out why on earth Aaron was not only here but also dressed like a caddy.

Something was not adding up, and I might not like calculators all the time, but I at least liked my numbers to make sense.

Chapter 21

The more I thought about it, the more I doubted it was Aaron out at the eighteenth hole. He had seemed pretty torn up about it all, and I'd kept him out late last night with the bird-watching. He was probably still home in bed.

So who was out in his golf cart, and why were they dressed as a caddy?

Unless it was Janina and she'd been playing me this whole time. It wasn't completely out of the realm of possibility. And if she had thought she'd get Leo's money after he died, it could make double sense. Plus, the body had looked more feminine than old-guy masculine.

But I was getting ahead of myself.

I crept through the trees on the outskirts of the course, trying to be as quiet as possible. I should know how to do this like a pro by this point with all my practice since Wednesday. But I was extra careful because I did not want to startle whoever was out here. And I certainly didn't want to make myself known until I was good and ready.

Creeping was not my forte, though, and so I had to go extra slow. It seemed like every time I put my foot down I snapped a twig or rolled a rock. Thank goodness I was at least wearing sneakers instead of the sandals I'd originally chosen this morning.

I got to the spot where the golf cart was left but didn't see anyone around. The chemical scent of flowers wafted toward me and I slowly breathed it in. The same scent I'd caught at Sylvie's out back, and the floral undertone I'd sniffed on the morning Leo had been found dead. I had thought it was just one of the guys with a different cologne on that day, and then perhaps the bush I was hiding in outside Sylvie's restaurant, but maybe it wasn't.

Maybe it was Elizabeth Arden's Red Door.

I could tell from the bumper stickers that the cart belonged to Aaron, but a female caddy had definitely been driving it earlier. So was it Janina? Or was it Sylvie? I knew who I'd rather it be.

And I wasn't surprised when I hid behind a tree that had a limited view of where the caddy was and saw a woman pick something black up off the ground. She shoved it into her pocket and then jumped in the golf cart and tore away, almost knocking an early golfer over.

I leaned back against the tree, not sure what to do now. Was it actually Sylvie? I wouldn't have been able to definitively pick her out of a lineup at the sheriff's station, but who else could it be? So, did I try to overtake the woman and demand to know what she'd removed from the ground?

Could whatever she had taken be the murder weapon? I still wasn't positive what had killed Leo, suicide or not. I wondered if Barney had a ready excuse and some lab tests to back up his story, because it couldn't have been a gun, and he hadn't hanged himself.

I took my time walking along the edge of the tree line to see if I could find anything that the police might have missed in treating this as a suicide instead of a crime scene. I wanted to make a beeline to the place where the woman had picked up the black thing from the ground, but just in case she hadn't left, I didn't want to appear obvious. Taking out my notebook and my phone, I pretended to take pictures of the flora and fauna of the area. The fake grass was as green as it ever was and the wild flowers along the tree line danced in the wind that rolled up from the ocean. Surprisingly enough, I found one of our rocks against the base of a tree. At least this one was a beautiful sunset with waves crashing against a sandy beach and not another threat.

I put it in my pocket and made plans to drop it off somewhere else later.

About a half an hour later, I made my way back to the main building. I hadn't found anything important, but I was glad that I'd at least taken the time to look it over. I wouldn't have been able to follow whoever had been in that cart, but I had some ideas on how to find out without putting up a chase.

It didn't take me nearly as long to get back to the main desk and there I found Bethany again.

"Hey, I forgot to tell you that I was interested in taking out a golf cart today, if you have one to spare. Something happened to my tires and I need to be able to scoot around today while it's getting fixed. Any chance of a loaner?"

"Sure, you can take the one around the corner since it doesn't seem like Janina's going to show up today." She shrugged and offered me the keys—just as I felt a rush of wind from the door behind me. Janina came running in, yelling that she was sorry she was late.

Leaning against the counter, she took a second to catch her breath and I took a moment to look her over. Same caddy uniform that I'd seen before, but different hair and different scent. She wore something spicy with a little kick, and her hair was reddish instead of the dark brown Sylvie sported. So unless she had put a wig on to come up and get something from the grounds, then she had not been the one driving that cart.

"Bethany, can I borrow Janina for a minute?" I looked Janina up and down, again trying to weigh her loyalty to her aunt against her desire to find out who had killed the love of her life. It could go either way, and I had to be prepared for both.

"I really need her to clock in, Whit, she had a party that's been waiting for her for about ten minutes." She gestured behind me, to where a pair of men sat with frowns on their faces. They didn't look like Aherns or Franklins so I ignored them to make my case.

"Two minutes is all I need, and I'll pay for the guys' caddy fees for today if they'll let me have her for five."

Bethany made eye contact with the two and spread her hands out to her sides.

The men conferred and then waved to Bethany.

"Okay, you have five minutes."

"Thank you." I turned to Sylvie's niece and hoped I hadn't been wrong about her. "Follow me."

She did, but reluctantly at first. I took her outside the building and over to the cart I would be borrowing for the afternoon. I sat on the seat sideways and tried to think about how to broach this whole subject, what I needed to know, and how to get it.

"Look, Janina, I'm going to be straight with you, and then you're going to do with the information whatever you want. I don't have time to beat around the bush because I have to get to the coroner before he gets to the police station, so I'm just going to spit it out, and then we'll go from there." I almost sounded like Maribel on one of her tangents. When I realized that, I stopped myself and drew in a deep breath.

"I'm pretty sure I saw your aunt here this morning, picking up something from the ground out by the eighteenth hole. She appeared to be wearing your uniform."

There was a moment of stunned silence. I let it sit between us without trying to break it.

"So, *that's* why I couldn't find my uniform this morning!" she said in a mini-shriek. "I asked her where it was and she told me to take a shower while she looked for it. When I got out of the shower she was running up the stairs in a bathrobe and locked herself in her room, telling me to fix my hair and she'd be out in a second. And then she came out with my uniform." She paced next to the cart, agitation radiating off her like the heat from a convection oven. "I didn't have time to care what she was doing because I didn't want to get in trouble for the second time this week for not being here on time. So I got dressed and left."

"What other day were you late?" I felt like I was on the precipice of something.

"The day Leo died."

We stared into each other's eyes for a few seconds, until she glanced down and a tear leaked out of her eye.

"Please, don't tell me . . ."

I stroked her arm. "I'm not going to tell you anything just yet. Let me dig a little deeper and see if I can get anything concrete, and then we'll go from there. I think my hunch is right, but I don't want to say anything until I know for sure. And our five minutes is up. Do your best to act as if nothing is wrong today. I'll get this wrapped up and come back to talk to you." I turned the ignition on in the cart. "Actually, would you be able to make a dinner cruise tonight, or are you working at the restaurant?"

"I'm not working, and I don't know if I'll ever be able to work there again if what you think is true."

"Like I said, I don't know anything for certain. I'm just trying to connect all the dots in the most logical way."

Another tear rolled down her cheek so I got out of the cart and I gave her a hug.

"Let me know when you have something concrete." Her words were muffled in my shoulder but I'd heard her.

"Promise," I said and then got back in my seat and put the cart in gear.

I stopped around the corner at the front desk again and gave Bethany my business credit card to pay for the men's round of golf. I'd figure out a way to claim it as an expense if I had to. For now it was all I had on hand and I needed to get to the docks.

There were throngs of visitors coming off the *Catalina Express* when I got there. I parked down a little ways, hoping that I'd be able to spot the coroner, Dr. Malloy, as he exited the cruiser. I'd looked him up online last night just to get his picture situated in my head. I hoped it wasn't a forty-year-old picture and that he still had the same haircut.

Otherwise I'd be lost.

I looked past the many people in their shorts, toting roller suitcases or golf bags behind them, and scanned the crowd. Unfortunately what I saw made my stomach turn. Barney was here and probably looking for the same person. I ducked behind my cart while I tried to rethink my way through this.

Nothing came to me. I couldn't exactly sneak around Barney. The coroner didn't know me so it wasn't like I could sideswipe him away from Barney as if we were old friends.

I popped up to see if there were any strategic places where I could grab him. Then I saw contact had already been made and my chance was lost. I was not going to be able to grab the coroner because Barney already had him in hand. I would have recognized him and been able to talk to him, but not with Barney on the prowl. Shit.

Now what was I going to do?

I quick-texted Maribel.

ARE YOU IN THE STATION?

YES. She came back quickly and in the affirmative.

I CAN'T GET TO CORONER. CAN YOU STAND OUTSIDE THE ROOM TO HEAR WHAT'S GOING ON?

MAYBE. FILING DONE BUT I'LL HAVE TO SNEAK.

YOU CAN DO IT, I texted back with a smiley face. She returned with an emoji sticking out its tongue.

It was going to have to be enough. My plan was thwarted, and I wasn't sure what would happen next.

I got a call from Goldy as Barney walked by my cart. He smirked in my direction and I wanted to kick my tire. Shit again!

"What's up, Goldy?"

"Well, I opened the shop a little early to grab the people coming in off the boat. I didn't know if you wanted me to do anything in particular while I'm standing in here? It seems Felix, Nick, and your grandfather must have come in here like house elves last night and fixed everything. It looks beautiful, in case you were wondering."

"Oh, thank goodness. I have to remember to thank them. I wish I'd known. I just saw Felix, but I didn't know they had done all that and he didn't mention it. I thought you could arrange some things around the shop, but if it's all done, then I guess just stand there and look pretty."

She chuckled and I smiled on my end. It was the last time I thought I'd do so for the rest of the day while all this went down.

"I'm not going to get to talk to Dr. Malloy, the coroner," I told her. "And now I don't know if I can get him to have an open mind about this autopsy."

"That's horrible. Can you get someone in on the inside? Do you know any of the doctors that might be with him?"

"No. No, I don't know anyone, and I can't call in a favor this late in the game. I should have thought about that earlier." I told Goldy I'd talk to her later and hung up. Why had I thought this would all work the way I wanted it to just because I wanted it to? Damn!

I took a few deep breaths while running several scenarios through my poor little brain. Nothing made sense, and I hadn't realized how much I had put my full stock into this working.

Closing my eyes didn't help a lot but it did give me just a second to sit with the information I had and what I still needed. I needed to know what Sylvie had picked up in the woods. I needed to know why she had picked it up and if she was the one who killed Leo.

There was a part of me that wanted it to be her just because I felt she had dealt Aaron a bad hand and seemed to be using her niece for cover all while hiding a husband no one knew about.

So had she killed Leo with whatever she had picked up and then ran him over with a cart by accident?

Had she stolen that cart from Aaron? Did she have a key to his garage or some way to get in that he didn't know about?

I grabbed my notebook out of my bag to write my questions down. I had a direction and I just had to hope that Maribel could get into position, and that the coroner was not an idiot.

Other than that I had people to talk to and things to learn. I also had a dinner party to set up, and I knew just who to set it up for now.

I called Aaron first and asked about his garage.

"No one can get in there," he said gruffly.

"Obviously they can if someone has gotten in there twice. Did you notice your cart gone again this morning?"

There was a pause and a door closed, then grumbling and some swearing. "It's parked wrong again."

"You're not going to be happy with this, but Sylvie had it this morning. I saw her out on the golf course. Can you look in it and see if she dropped anything?"

"Nothing in here that shouldn't be, but a few things are missing."

"Like what?"

"She took my keys."

"If you find anything else, please let me know."

"Sure. It's not too early to drink, is it?" He sounded so dejected I hated to ruin it further.

"I'm sure it's five o'clock somewhere. I'll come check on you later."

"Sure."

And he hung up. I felt horrible. But I also felt some little bubble of hope that I was getting close.

I headed back over to the golf course in my loaner cart and found Janina on the greens.

The guys she was driving around in another cart gave me a death glare when I interrupted her at the next hole, but they'd have to get over it. I'd paid for that cart.

"Janina, when Sylvie gave you your clothes, were they clean?" It could be a long shot, but it was worth asking.

"There was a stain on the knee, but I thought that was just from the other day. I did find these keys in the pocket, though." She dug in her backpack and handed over a key ring with a bunch of bird charms hanging off the ring. Aaron's keys; I could just tell these were his. And if she'd left those, had she also left the murder weapon in a pocket?

"Anything else? Something black?"

"Nope." She turned her pockets out and I felt deflated. I really wanted Sylvie to have forgotten both. I wanted to know what that murder weapon was. I could then present it to the coroner and they'd have to look deeper regardless of Barney.

"Where is Sylvie now?"

"She's at the restaurant preparing for your dinner party tonight."

A thought came to me and I felt like I really was the queen of dirty playbooks by asking. But it was worth the question.

"Would you at all consider going back to the house and seeing if there's something in her room that's black and square, I think? It should fit in the palm of your hand."

She bit her lip and looked at the ground. "I don't think I could do that."

"Even if it was the murder weapon?"

Her head snapped up, and I was afraid I'd overstepped. "Is that what you think she was out there getting?"

The anger in her voice could be at me or at her aunt, but I was in this far so I figured it couldn't hurt to go all the way. "Yes, I think she went out there this morning in your uniform so no one would pay attention to her going into the woods. And you have the proof in your hand that she took Aaron's golf cart. And that's the golf cart that ran over Leo. Aaron swears he didn't do it. Plus, he would have had to back over him to get the cart where it was when we found him, and the tracks only went one way."

She folded her lips in and looked like she was about to scream at me. Instead she surprised me by grabbing me in a big hug and bawling her eyes out.

"I'm scared, and I'm sad." She sobbed into my shoulder.

"I know, sweetie, but we have to give him justice. I'll take the guys around the rest of the course; it's almost done anyway. Run to the house and look around. Come back and if we're still on the course we can switch places."

"Okay. Okay, I'll do it. Leo needs justice and if it was Sylvie then she's going to pay like she will not even believe."

She handed me a sheet with numbers on it, handed me Aaron's keys, and ran off into the woods.

I hoped Sylvie was where she was supposed to be so that I hadn't just sent that poor girl into the murderer's den.

Chapter 22

An hour later, I hadn't heard from Janina but I had managed to not kill the two golf players as they took forever to golf and talk and basically waste my time. But I'd promised, and I'd come through. I worried about Janina but she could still be looking.

I explained to Bethany that I'd asked her to run an errand for me, and the front desk clerk had shrugged.

"She doesn't have anything else to do today and Daddy is off island, so I don't care what she does."

Okay, then. One thing down, a hundred more to go.

I had a lot of irons working in the fire and the next one I needed to poke the coals with was Goldy.

I breezed in to the store just as a set of four was walking out, marveling at their new rocks.

"Seriously. We're going to become the rock shop, aren't we?" I plopped my backpack on to the counter and shook my head.

"Would that be so bad? Then again it might be a fad and gone as quickly as it rocketed. Who knows? Enjoy it for the moment it's here, though, my darling. Things go so much better when you immerse yourself in the now instead of the past or too far into the future." Goldy hugged me and whispered in my ear, "Thelma was looking for you earlier. She doesn't trust cell phones, says that Big Brother is watching and she needs to talk to you. She's at her house, if you want to drop by."

I nodded and put that on my mental list, maybe next, after I handled business here. "In the meantime, I have an idea that I need you to run with and give it your all."

"Do tell." She leaned on the counter with her upturned hand cupping her chin.

"What do you think about inviting both families to the cruise tonight? Not all of them, but enough of them to fill the thing. Don't tell the other family who is also coming and just say that you're doing it to make up for my failure to the Franklins and as an apology for my bad behavior to the Aherns."

She clicked her tongue. "That has distinct possibilities, but why would I do that?"

"Because I'm pretty sure I know who did this, and I want both sides to hear it. Plus, I know what the family feud was about, and I think we can put an end to it."

She beamed at me. "Do tell!"

"I can't right now. This fire is burning super bright but I promise I will tell you everything before we get on the boat tonight, and I won't tell anyone else until I do. I want to have it all lined up before I spout off any more theories."

The beaming turned to scowling, but luckily I was saved by a customer coming into the store, asking about the rocks and if they could paint their own.

I left her to it, making a quick exit before she could catch me, and went straight to Thelma's.

My knock went unanswered so I tried again. I really hoped nothing had happened to her between her trying to get me and me coming to get her. What if Sylvie had hurt her? What if she'd followed her, heard that she had information, and hit the old woman with Aaron's golf cart? It seemed to be her M.O. at this point anyway.

But I knocked again just in case, and finally Thelma came to the door with a gooey face mask on and a scowl showing through the pink cream. "You could've called first. What if I'd been entertaining a gentleman for lunch?"

I glanced at my watch and found that it was noon. Why hadn't Maribel contacted me yet? How long did an autopsy take? Probably hours. I needed information if I was to be able to call the decision of the coroner into question.

"Sorry, I have a feeling that's not what you're doing, though, so can we just get to the info you have? I don't want to be rude, but I have a lot to do today. I also have a murderer to catch."

She harrumphed at me and squinted her creamed eyes. What did she want from me? A bow? A gift? Begging? I couldn't do any of the above unless she told me something new. I did, however, give her the rock out of my pocket and that made her smile in her weird cream mask.

"Fine, but we shouldn't do this out on the porch. Come in. I know you have places to be and things to do, but you can come in for one minute. I have cookies that you can take to your grandmother for me and that can be your reason for the visit, since I don't think you've ever been here before. You know, in case someone sees you leaving."

That was awesome thinking, so I hustled into the crammed front room and stood with my hands flat against my side. Her house was filled with dolls—in every shape and size and from every year, it looked like. She had old ones, new ones, small ones, and huge ones. Ones that I was pretty sure walked and talked. I did not want to accidentally touch any of them. I was absolutely certain that they would haunt my dreams.

"I got you a couple of pictures of the man you were looking

for." She came back out of the kitchen where I hadn't realized she'd disappeared to.

Her words hit me in the solar plexus and I gasped when she handed me a set of pages obviously printed off her computer.

"How did you get these?" It was the only question I could think of as my mind tried to process what I was seeing.

"I like to bird-watch early in the morning, and since last night was a bust I decided to go check out the front door of Sylvie's house at four this morning to see what was what. Didn't take long for that man to come creeping out the backyard. He didn't even have the decency to use the front door. But he had parked out front, so I waited for him to look in my direction and then started snapping like the paparazza I used to be. I still got it, in case you were wondering."

And she did. Each picture was a perfect angle and used the little light available in the neighborhood. I had a side view, a front view, a view of his boots, and a view of him getting into the golf cart, along with his license plate and dirt or something muddy on his tires.

Every picture showed George Martin in stark, vivid color, and they all made me rethink my whole plan.

Taking the cookies to Goldy, I made sure to sneak into the store while customers were shopping, leave them on the counter, and then whisk back out before she caught me.

I texted Janina a vague message to see if she'd found anything. I then sent a more pointed text to Maribel, who responded that Barney and Dr. Malloy were still looking over files and hadn't even gone to the morgue yet.

That was fine with me.

I strolled by the restaurant to see if Sylvie and her *husband* were hard at work getting my dinner together for the cruise tonight. They were, and that meant that at least Janina was still safe from being found.

Man, George was Sylvie's husband. I couldn't quite wrap my mind around it. What had she been thinking, and was that who she was talking about feeling like dirt with? That she would have chosen Aaron if not for George, or Raul, if you wanted to believe his driver's license and his rental agreement with the Middle Ranch. According to the receptionist when I called to ask if I could get lessons from him, he mucked at night and first thing in the morning.

So was he shoveling manure at other places too? And had he been in on the Leo Frankin thing just because he was married to an Ahern? Was he the one who'd left that "rock" on my front seat? I just wasn't sure. He had to have known about Aaron, though; he and Sylvie had talked about it in the back of her restaurant.

And I remembered that he'd also said that Leo was one thing taken care of. So had he been the actual killer? But how had he gotten Aaron's golf cart?

I was walking down the alley adjacent to the restaurant where I'd first hidden in the gardenia bush when my phone buzzed in my pocket. Thank goodness I'd turned it on silent. Especially when I saw a cloud of smoke come through the bush.

I quickly turned the other way and walked back to the grocery store where I'd left my loaner golf cart to answer it.

"Hey, you got tires now, if you want to come by." Manny, that old coot, might not work as a mechanic anymore but he'd agreed to put tires on for me at no charge when I decided I really couldn't wait for them to show up on their own at some later date.

"Give me a few. I have to run the loaner back to the golf course and then I'll stop in."

"Fine by me. Bring that Aaron with you. We have a few things to talk about, and I'd like a referee to keep it honest and hands off."

I rolled my eyes because I most certainly didn't want to be a referee between the two of them—or anyone, for that matter. But the other side of me felt like I owed it to both of them for trusting me and helping me, even if it was Thelma who finally handed me what I needed.

"It's going to have to be in about an hour, then," I said.

"I'll be here with my boxing gloves on."

I groaned as he hung up.

Boxing gloves and the two of them did not make for something to look forward to.

I needed more than anything to hear from Maribel now and know that the autopsy was not going in Barney's favor. I sent her a quick text but she didn't respond right away so I went on to the next thing.

Clearing my throat and taking a few deep breaths, I called the restaurant and asked to talk to Sylvie. I wanted to confirm that we were still on for the dinner and if she accidentally let slip why she had been out at the golf course so early this morning, I certainly wasn't going to turn away that information.

"Hey, Whit. Thanks for checking in. Yes, I have everything you need and we'll be ready tonight. Do you need servers?"

She did have everything I needed, including whatever she had picked up in the forest this morning, but I passed that thought out of my head and answered her question. "Actually, I don't think we need more than having the setup done. Unless you want to send a couple of people."

"No, that's okay. I'm hoping we'll be busy tonight, so I might only be able to spare myself and possibly George for setup."

"No free drinks this afternoon?"

She laughed, but there was a slight edge to it. "Yeah, no more free drinks. I think the promotion to get people in here worked fine for what it was worth, and now we have to go back to the old ways."

There was so much to unpack in there that I didn't know where to start. No more free drinks because she wasn't getting further money from Aaron, and therefore didn't need to launder it through her business anymore?

And the reference to the old ways. Was that a reference to her going back to just being with her husband, George—the guy who didn't even live with her and apparently didn't treat her well?

Regardless of what she'd meant, we signed off with a final goodbye and a promise to see each other later. I had plans to put together and needed to make sure Goldy was doing what I'd asked.

"How's it going there?" I said when she picked up the phone.

"This rock thing is getting a little out of hand. I'm almost out and I might have to go paint some more of my own. Who knew people would be so into dropping rocks along their walk? I had someone buy seven earlier. I don't know if the local government is going to be okay with this if every rock on the island ends up being painted."

"I'm sure it will be fine, and like you said it will probably die down as people find and move the rocks that are already out there. Any other business to report?"

"If you're asking about the families being invited, then might I just pat myself on the back for a moment and tell you that not only did I get Aaron Franklin and his family, including Leo's mom, to come, but I also managed to snag Fred Ahern and even Barney. The chief was very pleased that you'd seen the error of your ways and that an apology was forthcoming."

"Of course he was. Jerk."

"Don't say that too loud. Hold on a sec."

I heard a muffled conversation and then Goldy came back excited.

"Janina's here and she says she needs to see you right away

and that she might have to hide out at your house for a few days after what she found. Get down here."

She hung up on me before I could even ask what she was talking about. But that didn't stop me from jumping into my golf cart and wending my way through our streets and throngs of visitors to get to the Dame of the Sea gift shop.

I jerked to a stop at the curb and hopped out of the cart. Running seemed like a bad idea with another boat having just dumped its load of tourists. So I walked calmly into the store and then also very calmly waited for Goldy to handle a purchase of ten rocks before I stepped up to the counter.

"Where is she?" I asked quietly.

She hooked a thumb over her shoulder toward the back room.

I didn't waste any time opening the door and then quickly and quietly closing it behind me.

"Janina?" There was no one else in the room with me, but the door to the alley was slightly ajar.

I cracked it open a little further and found her standing outside, huddled against the wall and holding some object I didn't recognize. Peeking around the door, I wondered if she was cowering from someone, but there was no one else out here.

"Janina, what's going on? Why are you out here?"

She turned a tear-streaked face to me. "She really did it. She killed my fiancé. I went along with your theory at first because I thought for sure you had to be wrong, and I'd prove that you were wrong. But I just got a call from the sheriff's station and they think Leo was injected with horse tranquilizer and then tased. He would have probably died from the overdose but the Taser tripped his heart condition and made his system shut down. We'll have to wait for the toxicology report on the tranquilizer but the syringe injection site and some of the injuries indicate it's possible." She cried some more and I put my arm around her shoulders.

"I'm so sorry. I really didn't want it to be true. I like Sylvie or I did before all of this. But we have to do what brings justice to Leo."

"I want my old life back, Whit. Why does everything I love have to turn into manure?" She handed the Taser to me and then hugged herself hard enough to bruise her own ribs.

Her comment struck something in the back of my brain. Manure. Where had Sylvie gotten a horse tranquilizer and why had she decided to administer it to Leo, who was about three times her size? And why hit him with a Taser after he'd been dead? One more connection to George . . .

I hugged Janina to me one more time and then told her to head up to my house, where she could cuddle Whiskers if the cat would let her. I'd handle things and by tonight it would all be over.

It was a big promise, but I had a feeling I knew what had gone down. Now I just needed to prove it without a shadow of a doubt that Barney could try to hide inside.

Chapter 23

After I had texted Maribel again for confirmation on what Janina had told me, I walked to pick up Aaron at his house. I'd dropped off my loaner cart at the golf course as soon as I sent Janina to my house, without thought as to how I'd get around after that. But walking wouldn't hurt me.

Aaron had been reluctant to go with me to Manny's, but I'd promised to protect him. Not that I really thought I could keep Manny from raging if he wanted to. Maybe I could at least keep the confrontation to a minimum.

"We'll take my cart since everyone else seems to be driving it around lately. That way you can zip off as soon as you have yours and get the murderers."

"Why do you think it's plural and not just one murderer?" I asked. I'd been thinking the same thing myself, but I wanted to know why he thought so.

"Because there's no way that one person could have taken down Leo. He was a big guy and he would have fought. Maybe one of them ran him over with my cart and then once they had him on the ground they killed him, but I don't think one person could have done that much damage to my boy."

"Was he actually 'your' boy, Aaron?" Something had been

niggling at the back of my brain about their relationship, and how much more invested he'd seemed as more than just an uncle. Like the way Leo's mother, Judith, had turned into Aaron's arms when we'd seen her at the golf course and said that their boy was gone. He'd spent hours upon hours with that kid and then had brought him to his home when he'd come back to make his life better. He'd also been trying to help him leave to be with his girlfriend.

And then there was the fact that Aaron had never married.

Aaron glanced away and seemed to not want to answer, but then he looked back toward me and nodded. "One summer Judith and I got close when Sylvie had told me that there was no way we could be together. It was the summer after graduating high school. We slept together and then Leo came along and Judith decided to stay with my brother instead of leaving him to be with me. Story of my life, I guess. But at least I'd been allowed to be with him and be a father to him in so many ways. My brother never figured it out, not even before he died, and the secret was fine with me. All I wanted was for Leo to be healthy and have a good life. And now he has nothing—and neither do I." He shook his head. "Look, I'm depressed enough about everything that's going on. I'd rather go duke it out with Manny about my shortcomings than bring up all this history. Let's go."

He pulled his cart out of the garage and shook his head again at the damage to his garage door. "I'll have to fix that, I guess. Manny has a harder head than even I would have guessed."

I forced a laugh at what I thought was supposed to be a joke and hopped into the golf cart passenger seat, only to be jabbed in the butt by something.

Aaron started pulling out of the garage and I yelled for him to stop. He jerked to a halt and the thing jabbed me in the butt again.

Getting out of the cart, I stuck my hand into the crack between the back and seat bottom and came out with a capped syringe with the logo for Middle Ranch on it. "Holy heck, I think Manny's going to have to wait."

After sending Aaron back into the house for a plastic baggy, I called Maribel.

"Oh, man, thank you so much for picking up!" I said.

"What do you need, Whit? I'm still trying to get more information. Barney's trying to say that Leo could have injected himself with the tranquilizer and then he'd stun-gunned himself so that he wouldn't feel it. But they can't find the stun gun or the syringe, so the coroner is holding things up."

"I've got the syringe but I found it in Aaron's golf cart. I've also got the Taser, but I can't really say how I got that other than someone handed it over to me."

"That's not good. I've heard some rumblings that if Barney can't get it to be ruled a suicide, he's going to say Aaron killed Leo and tried to blame it on the other family."

"No, I can sew all that up. Look, can you stall them a little longer? Maybe get someone to recommend that the investigation and the autopsy findings be held off until after the pieces are found? I think I can get this all out into the open tonight, but I need Barney and the coroner at the boat this evening for dinner. Barney's already a solid yes, since he thinks I've changed my ways and the dinner is an apology to the Aherns for my failings. Can you get the coroner to come?"

"He's not bad looking," she mused. "If I can get an invite, I could probably invite him as my date. I didn't see a ring on his left hand, anyway."

"That's my girl. Work on that and I'll get back to you. The boat is leaving the dock at six this evening, so I have about an hour to get things ready before I have to meet the murdering caterers. Can you see if we can get everyone down there by five-thirty?"

"Will do. Don't forget to invite Felix too. He might like to be in on the action."

"He's my next call—because I might need additional backup if this goes horribly sideways."

The inside of the *Sea Bounder* was set up just the way I wanted it. Nick had come when I'd asked and had agreed to help, though he thought I was going overboard. Hopefully not literally, but he thought I was trying too hard. He could keep his opinions to himself.

I had all the blinds pulled over the windows and Felix helped me remove the furniture from the open back deck so that George and Sylvie, in all their murderous glory, could set up the buffet out there in an hour. Per my plan, they thought they were getting here before everyone else, but that was not what was actually going to happen. Not at all.

I walked up the dock at a little before five to get a few more supplies, and when I came back after a stop at the store I heard chaos before I even managed to get to the sidewalk leading to the dock.

"You aren't supposed to be here!" I heard shouted as I stumbled along the gravel.

"I'm not the one who's not supposed to be here, *you're* not supposed to be here! This is a private cruise so we can figure out which one of you killed Leo!"

Uh-oh.

"No one killed Leo. He was a coward and took the coward's way out. No one at fault but him—and your family for not taking care of your own."

I winced when what I had hoped wouldn't happen happened. Someone shoved someone else and off the edge of the dock they went.

Felix was in motion before I could even ask him to save whoever it was that had gone into the drink.

I threw myself into the melee as the others on the dock started in on one another.

"No, no, no! We're not doing this here. Besides, there's only one rescue diver, and I'm not going to have him exhausted because of your continued stupidity." I put my arms out to keep them all away from one another and turned in a continuous circle to keep my eye on as many as I could.

What was wrong with these people? I'd never seen them outwardly aggressive to each other. Hell, I hadn't even known about any kind of feud until Leo was found, and now it was erupting like a dormant volcano that had a lot to spew from being pent up for so long.

"Someone answer this question," I said, eyeing each of them and slowing my circle because I was getting dizzy and did not want to be the next one to fall into the water. I caught Felix out of the corner of my eye boosting whoever had been pushed into the water up the ladder on the side of the dock.

They all stopped grumbling and actually looked at me. I stepped to the end of the two very separate lines of combatants and took their measure. We had young and old, short and tall, male and female. I wanted answers and didn't care who gave them, so I moved my gaze from one side to another and went down the line, not letting anyone out of my sight and not focusing on anyone in particular.

"What's the question?" Fred Ahern growled.

"Let the girl think. My God, not everything has to be done just because that's what you want and when you want it." Becca Franklin crossed her arms over her small chest and jutted her chin out at the other side.

"Look, we are not going to fight about my question. I have a feeling you don't need any more reasons to despise one another. So here's the question: Who knows what the original feud was over, and why is it still going on?"

"That's two questions." I got that from the left, but couldn't tell who had said it since the right was yelling that they should just be quiet.

"Everyone shut it!" Judith, Leo's mom, yelled as she stepped out in front of everyone else and stood right in front of me. I was happy to see her here. Goldy had told me she was coming, but I hadn't been positive that she would really show when she was still grieving the death of her son.

"Are you sure you want to be here in the midst of all this?" I asked.

"If nothing else, I will get them all to settle down. I'm tired of all the up-in-arms about everything." A tear slid down her face and she turned her head toward the ocean at my back to whisk it away. Clearing her throat, she faced me again. "Good luck getting anyone to talk about the feud, because no one knows why it started, and no one wants it to end if all these ya-hoos are anything to go by. They refuse to talk to each other and the hatred is so ingrained they're incapable of moving beyond it." With that she stomped off, obviously having said her piece and not wanting anything more to do with it.

But why the tears? Why was it so important to her to have things end if she couldn't stick around to see if this was the opportunity for everyone to finally talk it out?

I had no idea. And with the amount of huffing and puffing going on, I guessed it probably wouldn't end here anyway.

But Aaron caught her at the end of the dock and brought her back.

"Let's give this a chance and see what happens," he said as they rejoined the group.

"Oh, Aaron, what does it matter? He's gone and my life is over. I have nothing left."

"Of course you do, sweetheart." He stroked her hair and kissed the top of her head.

"While this is all very unenlightening, I'm sure I have better things to do." Barney Warrington turned to move off the dock, but Dr. Malloy grabbed his arm and brought him back in line.

"You're staying until this is explained. I have friends in

higher places than you can possibly know, Barney, and your handling of this so far is very much in question. If you leave now, I'll make sure you have no way of ever coming back."

The threat seemed to work because Barney stayed—with a sullen expression on his face, of course, but still he stayed.

"Okay, then, I have a cruise to run, so here's what we're going to do. You're all going to keep your mouths shut and get on board. You'll sit on either side of the windows because I doubt the poor *Sea Bounder* can handle all of you and your enormous hatred and egos seated next to each other."

I turned away to find Felix standing behind me, sopping wet. He flicked his hair out of his eyes with his fingers. "I might have to sit this one out. I'm soaked to the skin and I don't think you want me dripping in the cargo hold."

I waved toward the boat. "You're not getting off that easy. There's a spare set of pants and a company T-shirt in the front cabin. At this point, if they all kill each other, I'll just heave them to and the fish can dine al fresco this evening."

I tromped down the dock and figured people would follow if for nothing else than curiosity—and because they had free food from La Annaffiare to look forward to.

They had no idea what was coming with that food.

At this point, if I didn't already know who had killed Leo, I would have considered all of them suspects, even the younger ones. Who knew what vile and evil they were spoon fed along with their breakfast cereal?

Surprisingly enough, while I checked the engines and made sure that everything was a go for the boat ride, two lines of people filed on board and they sat in the rows like they had stood up on the dock. Angry glares were exchanged across the middle of the ship where the glass inserts had been placed into the floor to watch the sea life float and swim beneath us, but no one spoke. If even one of them damaged my boat, I was going to have them all hauled down to the jail.

Oh my, this was going to be a fun run if I ever had one, and the island was going to owe me big for not letting my passengers just kill each other and get it over with.

I heard metal rattling down the dock and turned to everyone in the darkened cabin. "Keep your mouths shut. Don't say a word until I tell you that you can." I stared at each one down the lines on both sides and when I didn't get any pushback I figured that was as good as it was going to get.

I fast-tracked my way to the back of the boat and quickly opened the sliding door, then closed it again behind me before the carts made it to the deck.

"Hey, Sylvie. Hey, George. Thanks for coming out. I'm hoping that we can get underway in just a bit, if you don't mind setting up out here. I think it will make for a good place. Everyone will be able to see the food as they get onboard. I'm sure they'll all be salivating by the time we get underway. I thought of putting covers on the wells in the bottom of the boat and placing the food there but then no one could see anything as we rolled by—at least nothing living in the sea, maybe some boiled crab cakes or a few lobster tails." I knew I was babbling but I covered it with a laugh and escorted them onto the boat with their rolling metal buffet carts. They had two, each with four metal dishes placed in the steaming water tables underneath.

"Whatever you need. And thanks for inviting us out like this. We haven't been on a cruise in a while," George said.

Sylvie glanced at him and then looked away. More trouble in what wasn't paradise to begin with? That could work in my favor.

"I'm just going to step off here to see if any of our passengers are coming along. I've invited the Aherns and the Franklins to dinner tonight to see if we can't work out their differences. I found out what the feud is about this afternoon after a ton of digging around. I think a few apologies should turn things around. Especially now that the cause of death has been confirmed."

I walked off the boat and tried not to look behind me to see what was happening. Instead I relied on the fact that I had switched on the speaker from the back deck to filter into the cabin and had a handheld walkie in my pocket to hear if they said anything incriminating.

"We can't be here when they all come on board." Sylvie's voice was low but extremely angry and scared, harsh even. I could see out of the corner of my eye that she kept her head down. From my peripheral vision I could just make out the movements of both of them.

George grabbed her arm and tilted her face up with a yank of his other hand. It could have been mistaken for an embrace if you didn't know the history there. But I knew better.

"Don't you dare get stupid again. Or is that stupider? You're the one who started this all in the first place. You could have just put Aaron off when he proposed marriage, or even got engaged and then demanded a huge wedding that could have taken years to put together. Instead you got all sentimental and didn't want to go through with it, and now we're stuck."

She yanked her arm away but he grabbed her again. She snarled and spit words at him. "And you were only supposed to stun Leo to get him to talk to Aaron about continuing to be the conduit for the money. But no, you went in there heavy-handed like you always do and you ruined it."

"You should have told me he had a heart condition," he shot back.

"And you shouldn't have tranquilized him so much to get him to sign some stupid suicide note if he didn't do what you said. You were just supposed to tase him." She stomped her foot and George let go. She must have hit his foot.

"Come on now, it would have all been fine if you hadn't

raced over in your boyfriend's golf cart and ran the poor bastard over to add insult to injury. Your uncle was all on board with making this a suicide but then you had to ruin it like you always do."

Listening to their exchange, I wondered what the reaction inside the cabin was. More, though, I hoped that Felix was keeping things under control. I also had Goldy and Nick on the inside and she would unleash on them if she had to.

I was pretty sure that was enough of a confession to keep things rolling in the right direction, so I strolled back to the boat and got on board. "Everything all set up?"

"Yep," Sylvie said with a strained smile. George gave me the stink eye, but didn't say a word.

"Okay, then, I think we're almost ready."

"We are not ready!" Aaron came bursting out of the cabin behind me. I thought I'd locked the door, but I might have forgotten that in my haste to get everything else right.

Aaron went for George hard and they both tumbled over the edge of the railing and into the drink. Felix was fast on his feet and got into the water for the second time in an hour. I didn't have more clothes to lend him, but from the expression on Barney's face when he slowly made his way out to the deck to face off with Sylvie, I didn't think some wet clothes were going to matter.

"So the whole feud had to do with death in the first place and now it's ended with death. How cosmically aligned can you get?" Reese put down the pen she'd been using to write out my story, or at least the pieces I'd been able to gather. We'd confirmed them with archives both at the hospital and in the police department and the files she had here at the newspaper.

"I'm just sad that both times it was a Franklin that had to die."

It was the next morning and justice was well on its way to being served. Barney was being demoted, Leo's death would be written up as a murder, George and Sylvie were on their way to jail, and I'd seen Aaron and Judith having breakfast this morning at the diner on my way to the paper.

I twirled my own pen on the notepad that had so much information in it that I might want to try my hand at writing a book.

"It is sad, but at least Delilah can be at peace now instead of written up as a drunk who took too many chances." Reese swiveled in her chair to look at the rows and rows of microfiche. "I wonder what other mysteries are in here. This can't be the only unexplained thing to happen on the island. Maybe I should dig in some more. See what I can find. I wouldn't mind a helper." She looked over her shoulder at me and I laughed.

"I might be taking you up on that since Goldy seems to be running my shop much more efficiently than I ever have, and the money is coming in hand over fist." I tapped my fingers on the tablet. "What do you think of all these rocks going on the island?"

"Honestly, I think it's a great idea. Everyone is enjoying themselves and you could even advertise on them if you really wanted to. Just put your website on the back or something."

It might just be worth running past Goldy. And since when did I have to run my decisions past her?

If I were also being honest, always. I depended on her. When your mother and father left without a word and never came back, you kind of had to look for someone else to fill the gap. Goldy had not only filled it, but had also overflowed like the whale in the tiny puddle.

And then there was Pops, who always had my back, and Maribel, who was the best friend a girl could ask for. My brother,

Nick, who might sometimes be a loose cannon, was a good guy all the same. Then finally there was Felix—Felix, who was waving to me from outside the archive room.

I waved back, said my goodbyes to Reese, picked up my notebook, and went to see what was next with a confidence I hadn't felt in a long time.

Don't miss how it all began in
MUCH ADO ABOUT NAUTICALING.
Available now
from Gabby Allan
and
Kensington Books
wherever books are sold.

Visit us online at
KensingtonBooks.com
to read more from your favorite authors,
see books by series, view reading
group guides, and more!

Visit us online for sneak peeks, exclusive
giveaways, special discounts, author content,
and engaging discussions with your fellow readers.

Betweenthechapters.net

Sign up for our newsletters and be the first
to get exciting news and announcements about
your favorite authors!
Kensingtonbooks.com/newsletter